J. T. EDSON'S
FLOATING OUTFIT

The toughest bunch of Rebels that ever lost a war, they fought for the South, and then for Texas, as the legendary Floating Outfit of "Ole Devil" Hardin's O.D. Connected ranch.

MARK COUNTER was the best-dressed man in the West: always dressed fit-to-kill. **BELLE BOYD** was as deadly as she was beautiful, with a "Manhattan" model Colt tucked under her long skirts. **THE YSABEL KID** was Comanche fast and Texas tough. And the most famous of them all was **DUSTY FOG**, the ex-cavalryman known as the Rio Hondo Gun Wizard.

J. T. Edson has captured all the excitement and adventure of the raw frontier in this magnificent Western series. Turn the page for a list of Floating Outfit titles.

J.T. Edson

THE FAST GUN

CHARTER BOOKS, NEW YORK

This Charter Book contains the complete
text of the original edition.
It has been completely reset in a typeface
designed for easy reading, and was printed
from new film.

THE FAST GUN

A Charter Book/published by arrangement with
Transworld Publishers, Ltd.

PRINTING HISTORY
Brown, Watson edition published 1967
Corgi edition published 1969
Berkley edition / May 1981
Charter edition / May 1990

ISBN: 1-55773-343-0

Charter Books are published by The Berkley Publishing Group,
200 Madison Avenue, New York, New York 10016.
The name "CHARTER" and the "C" logo
are trademarks belonging to Charter Communications, Inc.

PRINTED IN THE UNITED STATES OF AMERICA

10 9 8 7 6 5 4 3 2 1

CHAPTER ONE

The Son of a Prominent Citizen

The four young men in the General Sheridan Saloon looked like trouble, or the well-travelled and experienced bartender had never seen it. Although the wall clock's hands stood at only ten o'clock in the morning, the quartet showed signs of carrying enough Old Stump Buster to make them truculent. At the pool table, three of the four played a rowdy game and seemed to be doing their damnedest to cause mischief and damage. The fourth member of the group stood just inside the main doors and watched Bainesville's main street in the hope of finding fresh devilment into which he could steer his companions.

Tall, lean, wearing cowhand clothes, although without the tanned face long exposure to the elements gave most members of the cattle chasing profession, sporting an 1860 Army Colt in a low cavalry-twist draw holster, the street watcher's expression was one calculated to convince people of his salty, uncurried nature. Turkey Cooper wanted very much to build himself a name; and spent most of his waking hours working towards that end.

Like Turkey, two of the remainder spelled trouble to Western eyes. Clad in range clothing, looking like

1

cowhands to untutored eyes, their appearance fooled
nobody who knew the West. Looking a younger version
of Turkey, Coop Cooper cultivated his elder brother's
habits, although making sure that he never eclipsed
the other; to do so called down painful repercussions.
Shorter and slightly heavier built, Lanny Bulmer
followed the general style and habits of the brothers. All
in all, the trio looked and acted like many of the type
throughout the cattle country.

Maybe once in a while, when driven to it by force of
circumstances, their kind might take employment on a
ranch; but never stayed for long and mostly left under a
cloud. Their normal occupation consisted of loafing
about any town that would put up with them, joining in
any fun or fuss that happened to be going and terroris-
ing much of the citizens who failed to show courage in
facing them. Occasionally, when largesse from real cowhands did not come, such young men stepped over the
line and went outside the law, to meet a well-deserved
fate at the hands of a peace officer or posse.

The particular trio currently gracing Bainesville with
their presence had little danger at that time of being
forced into work or crime as a means of earning their
daily bread; having found a way to supply their needs
without raising either sweat or danger. In return for
their company and acceptance as their leader, the fourth
young man kept them in food, drink and free from
interference by the local law.

While as tall as Turkey Cooper, Gavin Gartree had a
slimmer build. If one discounted a sullen mouth and
narrow-set eyes, Gartree might be termed handsome.
Dressed to what he fondly imagined to be the height of
fashion, he too failed to fool people who knew the
range. Silver conchas glittered on the band of his costly
white Stetson, and a pure silk bandana knotted at his

throat trailed ends over his expensive shirt, almost to the waist band of his levis pants. The gunbelt around his waist had been designed for speedy withdrawal of the pearl handled Navy Colt in its holster and Gartree believed himself to be something of a master in its use.

Son of a wealthy, influential and prominent politician, Gartree was arrogant and possessed a vicious, carping sense of humor. His father, a man of "liberal" views, gave him everything he wanted—except for parental discipline—and used his influence in the small Kansas town to shield his son from the consequences of a number of rash actions.

Small wonder that Gavin Gartree found the three young men so willing to act as his companions and treat him as their leader.

Raising his cue almost perpendicular, Gartree stabbed hard at a ball and caused it to leap from the table. The tip of the cue forced up the green cloth's nap and left a white chalk mark, coming close to opening up a tear in the surface. Coop nudged Lanný, nodded in the direction of the bartender and winked. Moving to the side of the table, Coop bent, made a bridge with his left hand, sawed his cue back and forwards with the right and slammed the eight ball so that it tore along, struck the cushion in the corner and bounced clear over to land on the floor.

An angry grunt left the bartender's lips as he watched the two actions. In his employer's absence, the bartender had the responsibility of running the business. Yet he knew that the owner allowed Gartree's bunch a degree of latitude not extended to customers with less influential backing. It galled a man to stand watching a bunch of idle yahoos act up and yet be unable to take the appropriate action against them.

Ignoring the noise behind him, Turkey Cooper

remained at his post and watched the street. An exceptionally fine paint stallion stood at the hitching-rail of the barber's shop across the street; its low horned, double girthed range saddle a sure sign that a Texas man owned it. Bainesville lay to the east of the great interstate trails along which the Texans drove their herds to market, but Turkey had seen enough of those trail herding men to know that he must not try any of his games with the animal. From the fact that the saddle carried a tarp-wrapped bedroll strapped to its cantle, Turkey concluded that the paint's owner passed through rather than worked for a local outfit and came to town on a spree. Neither the coiled, hard-plaited Manila rope strapped to the saddlehorn, nor the Winchester Model '66 carbine in the boot were sufficiently out of the ordinary as to excite any comment.

While Turkey wondered if the Texan might be good for free drinks and fun later, he saw something which took his mind from thoughts of hoorawing the town. A much more satisfactory source of amusement had made its appearance; one he felt sure his three companions would wish to enjoy.

The wagon coming along Cresset Street looked little different from thousands of others which roamed the great open range country, carrying travellers and their belongings from place to place over the miles between the Mississippi River and the Pacific Ocean. Four good quality horses drew the wagon, although the man handling the reins had not the appearance of a hard-rock haulage driver. That the new arrivals attracted any interest among the few people who went about their business on Cresset Street was merely because it carried strangers and such could generally be counted on to bring news of other areas.

Not that Turkey Cooper watched the approaching

wagon with any desire for news behind his interest.

"Hey!" he called. "Come and take a look at what's coming."

At the pool table, Gartree and his companions had begun to despair of rousing the bartender to protests at their deliberate actions. Deliberately letting his cue fall to the floor and leaving it there, Gartree swaggered across the room towards the batwing doors. Tossing his cue on to the table so its tip struck the cushion hard, Coop directed a challenging grin in the direction of the fuming bartender who chose to ignore both actions. Lanny rested his cue on his shoulder and took it along as he followed on his companions' heels.

On reaching the doors, Gartree opened his mouth to ask why Turkey interrupted a most interesting game. He held down the question as his eyes followed the direction of Turkey's gaze and studied the occupants of the wagon.

Two men sat on the wagon's box and Turkey nodded towards them. "Who'd you reckon they are, Gav?"

"Look like Quakers, or some such," Coop suggested, studying the men's sober black suits, collarless shirts, round topped black hats and bearded, solemn faces.

"Sure looks that way," agreed Lanny. "Hey now! Just look at that!"

He did not need to give the advice, for eight eyes drank in the sight of the girl who emerged from the wagon's interior and stood behind the men. Small, petite, with a perfectly formed, beautiful face that bore an expression of wide-eyed innocence, the girl would have drawn admiring glances in almost any company. Although a sun bonnet covered her hair, she had the coloration of a blonde; and not even the severe lines of the black dress she wore could hide the rich fullness of the curves below.

"Now that's what I call a right pretty girl," announced Gartree and for once his companions' muttered agreement was not entirely sycophantic.

"Thing now being what're we going to do about her," commented Turkey, watching the wagon come alongside and then pass by.

"Shouldn't ought to let a pretty gal like that come to our fair city without us showing her some hospitality," Coop continued.

Most likely nothing would have come of the talk if the strangers continued on their way. The quartet's horses were at the livery barn, requiring collection and saddling before they could be used and none of Gartree's bunch cared to exert themselves unduly for their amusement. If following the strangers entailed any effort, the four would have returned to their efforts at baiting the bartender. However, the wagon halted outside Bixby's General Store, not more than one building's length from the saloon.

"Let's go down and make talk," Gartree ordered and pushed open the batwing doors.

Followed by his companions, Lanny still shouldering the pool cue, Gartree strolled along the sidewalk in the direction of the wagon. He watched the two men climb down, moving slowly and stiffly in the manner of those who travelled far on the hard box seat of a wagon. Due to having halted close to the store's hitching rail, the travellers had to alight on the wheel and hoof-rutted center of the street, looking around them with as much interest as if Bainesville was the first town they had ever seen.

Studying the newcomers as he approached them, Gartree noticed that neither of the men wore guns. The four young men halted on the sidewalk and Gartree hooked his forearm on the butt of his gun, supporting the upper part of his body and standing in what he imagined to be a relaxed, but ready and masterful posture. After examining the two male strangers again in an attempt to locate hidden arms, Gartree made his decision.

"I'll tend to it, wait here," he said, and swung off the sidewalk to walk by the heads of the wagon team.

A hint of annoyance furrowed Turkey's brow, for he hoped to have his share in the fun. However, he held his objections inside him, figuring that it might be better to miss some fun. One of the things Gartree expected in return for the money he spent on his companions was to have his own way in all things large and small.

Swaggering forwards Gartree approached the travellers and his face took on an expression of disarming charm that usually came as a prelude to an outbreak of what his father termed 'youthful high spirits'; but which less biased people gave a different and more apt name.

"This'll be good," grinned Lanny.

"Real good," sniffed Turkey. "Especially if those fellers show tough. Then we'll get called in quick enough."

"Howdy," Gartree greeted, halting before the trio and adopting his gun-leaning posture again to show them that they faced the real thing. "You folks come far?"

Although all three looked in Gartree's direction, none made any reply for a moment. It seemed that the elder of the male travellers—a venerable, white-haired and bearded man with a sober, intelligent cast of features—was thinking out the correct words to use before answering. Yet, when he finally spoke, his English, if a touch slow and precise, carried no trace of an accent.

"We have come a long journey. Could you please tell me the name of this town?"

"Bainesville, Kansas," replied Gartree with a broadening grin.

The possibilities of the situation improved by the minute. Not only did the travellers belong to some unimportant and obscure religious sect; but their leader appeared to be speaking in a foreign language. Such a combination offered almost limitless opportunities for fun of the most vicious kind; and that was the type Gartree liked when half drunk. From what he knew of the town marshal, Bainesville's only representative of law and order, Gartree expected no interference from that source no matter how he mishandled the newcomers.

"Bainesville, Kansas," repeated the elder man gravely and lapsed into silence for a short time. Although he stood looking straight into Gartree's face, the man gave no sign of being aware of the other's presence. At last he gave a slow nod of his head and continued, "So this is Bainesville, Kansas."

"Sure is," agreed Gartree, throwing a nod and wink in the direction of his watching companions. "How long're you staying here?"

Again came the slight pause as the old man collected his words, then he replied, "Perhaps we may stay for a time. It all depends on if we find what we came looking for."

"It's a fine little town," Gartree remarked, directing his words to the girl and stripping her with his eyes. "A whole lot of nice things happen here when I'm around."

Cool blue eyes studied Gartree with an infuriating indifference, for the local girls showed more interest in the son of the town's most prominent citizen. Fed on the respect—real or pretended—of people in Bainesville, nothing roused Gartree's anger more than a person who failed to accord him what he felt to be his due.

"I doubt if we will be staying here," the girl declared, speaking in the same precise manner as the man.

"Not even long enough to take a meal," asked Gartree.

"I think not," answered the girl definitely.

"Not even was I to offer to stand treat for all of you to the meal?" Gartree continued. "Of course you'll come with me, and the boys'll look after your pappy and grandpappy there."

The girl did not reply for a moment. From the puzzled expression on her face, Gartree guessed that she did not understand his colloquial speech and this amused him without lessening his anger at her indifference. A half smile played momentarily as she glanced at her two companions; then she became grave-faced as her eyes turned to Gartree's face once more.

"No, thank you," she declined.

"Tell you what," hissed Gartree, his anger growing at the refusal. "You come with me for a meal, and I'll join in your prayers before and after we eat."

"Prayers?" said the girl. "I don't understand you."

"Come on now," grinned Gartree. "All you glory-hunters pray real hard for the good Lord to give you what you want; and try to convert everybody to your ways."

"We have no wish to convert anybody," objected the girl. "Nor do we want anything at all."

"Now me," sneered Gartree, "I'm different, I want something. And whatever I want, I go right ahead and get it."

"What do you mean?" asked the girl, her expressive face showing a hint of concern as she moved closer to her companions.

"You know what I mean. I aim to take you for a meal."

Something in Gartree's tone and attitude must have

warned the girl against accepting his invitation, even if
she could not fully understand the meaning of his
words. Both her companions showed signs of their
concern and the younger threw a glance towards the
wagon. It was the elder man who made the next move.

"Get on to the wagon," he said to the girl. "I think
we will leave."

"And I think you won't!" Gartree spat out.

"But we wish to resume our journey," the girl said.

"And I wish for you to stay here," mocked Gartree.
"Which same, I'm a man who likes to see his wishes
come true."

"I do not understand," the girl replied.

"Maybe I'd best show you then," Gartree told her,
his lips twisting in a slobbering leer as he moved towards
the girl.

Opening his mouth as if to speak, the elder man took
a step forward so as to prevent Gartree reaching the girl.
Before the man could speak, Gartree laid the palm of
his hand against the bearded face and shoved hard. A
low mutter ran through the small crowd of townspeople
who had gathered on the sidewalks, but Gartree expected no interference from the local citizens. Throwing
a quick glance to make sure that his three companions
stood by ready to back his plan, Gartree reached towards the girl.

What had started out as nothing more than a piece of
horseplay suddenly changed. After seeing the old man
thrust aside, the girl stood without movement. Her face
lost all its previous expression, became an unreadable
mask, as she faced Gartree. An almost luminous glow
came into her eyes, discomforting Gartree; but not
enough to make him change his intentions.

Never before had Gartree's advances met with so little
response. Gartree read contempt and loathing in the

girl's blank expression, twisting it to give him an excuse for his next move. All his vicious nature, nurtured by a lifetime lacking in parental restraint, boiled up and drove him onwards.

Taking a stride which carried him past the elder man, Gartree reached out with his hands towards the girl. The blank mask wavered and went as the girl saw Gartree closing on her and he revelled in the sight of the shocked fright which replaced it. From the way she acted, the little blonde might have guessed what thoughts raced through Gartree's head. Panic came into her eyes as she felt his hands clamp hold of her arms. Then he felt her drawing back in an attempt to free herself. While the girl lacked the strength to pull herself free, she resisted his plan to drag her closer. Although she directed a pleading glance towards the younger of her companions, she neither screamed nor asked him to help. For all that, the man made as if to go towards the wagon and Gartree could guess for what reason.

"Watch him, Turkey, he's going to get a gun!"

"Just let him try it," Turkey answered in a tough voice.

Secure in the knowledge that he had protection against the traveller, Gartree turned his attention to the girl once more.

"Come here, you mealy-mouthed psalm singer," he ordered. "Let's see if you can kiss like a woman."

"R—Release me!" she gasped, still straining away from him.

"You heard the lady," put in a cold, authoritative voice from beyond the girl. "Get your cotton-picking hands off her."

CHAPTER TWO

Gavin Gartree's Mistake

Raising his head, ready to yell for assistance, Gartree looked to see what kind of man dare come between him and his desires. From the slow, easy drawl underlying the cold, commanding hardness in the voice, Gartree assumed that the speaker did not hail from Bainesville—nor was even a native of Kansas. What he saw filled him with a mixture of surprise, relief and fury.

The manner of speaking, like one long used to giving orders and receiving obedience without question, had led Gartree to expect a big, dangerous looking man to be responsible for the interruption.

Instead, he stared at a small, insignificant appearing Texas cowhand who crossed the street from the direction of the barber's shop. Setting a low-crowned, wide brimmed black Stetson hat on his freshly cut and combed dusty blond hair, the Texan strode purposefully forward. He was a handsome young man, if one took the trouble to look closely, but somehow did not catch the eye unless doing something unusual. Although his range clothing was of good quality, he lacked the ability to show it off and gave it the appearance of coming from the second-hand shelf of one of the cheaper general stores. Not even the finely made gunbelt around his

waist, or the two matched bone-handled 1860 Army
Colts riding butt forward in the shaped holsters made
the Texan look more dangerous or noticeable.

While it seemed highly unlikely that such a small
nobody would own so fine an animal, every sign pointed
to the huge paint stallion as belonging to the Texan. Not
that Gartree gave the horse a thought. Nor did he pay
any attention to the significant and distinctive manner
in which the small man's holsters had been built to the
contours of the guns. Gartree's eyes took in the Texan's
lack of size and general appearance of nonentity. Anger
at the interruption filled the young man and overrode
his normal caution; so he omitted to take his usual
precaution of calling in his three companions to handle
the situation. For once, Gartree figured that he could
fight his own battle.

"Just who in hell asked you to bill in," he snarled,
still retaining his hold on the girl and watching the
Texan come closer.

"I said let loose," answered the other, ignoring the
question.

Changing his expression to one of innocent mildness,
Gartree grinned amiably. "Anything you say, friend,"
he purred.

And saying it, Gartree thrust the girl away from him,
then threw what he fondly imagined to be a real good
punch at the Texan's head. Nothing about the Texan
hinted that he expected to be attacked and Gartree
figured that he had lulled the other's suspicions with his
brilliant acting.

At which point, the Texan proceeded to disillusion
Gartree in no uncertain way. Throwing up his left hand,
the Texan blocked and deflected Gartree's outlashing
right fist. Before Gartree recovered from the shock
handed by the failure of his attack, he found other

troubles heaped upon him. Small the Texan might be,
but he was muscled like a pocket Hercules and moved as
fast as a striking diamondback rattlesnake. A fist that
felt solid as a knob of iron ripped into Gartree's belly,
driving air from his lungs and in nausea which knotted
his guts in agony. Over doubled Gartree, croaking in
pain, ideally position for a further attack. From block-
ing the blow at his head, the Texan's hand swung down,
across his body and whipped upwards to drive the back
of his knuckles into the offered face. Head spinning as
mists clouded his eyes, Gartree came erect and sprawled
backwards to crash into the hitching rail.

Turkey gave out with a low growl as he saw Gartree
land almost at his feet. Realising that the other would
expect to hear, when capable of listening and understanding, that his friends extracted a painful
vengeance on his assailant, Turkey lunged forward.
Maybe at that moment Turkey remembered a licking
received at the hands of a Texan during a hectic visit to
the trail-end town of Newton. Or his motives could have
been the antipathy many Kansans felt towards supporters of the Confederate States; even though the War
ended some four years back. Loyalty to Gartree, or
rather the good things in life which the young man
represented, also gave Turkey real prime motivation;
but not enough for him to take chances. Having come
through a few roughhouse brawls against local boys and
emerged as victor, Turkey expected no trouble in
dealing with the Texan. If Turkey thought of the matter
at all, knowing how poorly Gartree showed on the rare
occasions when induced to fight, he put the Texan's success down to pure luck.

Moving fast, Turkey reached for the Texan and relied
on his weight to bear the other's resistance down and
smash him to the ground. Instead of trying to avoid the

rush, the Texan glided forward a pace and acted with the same speed already shown when handing Gartree a lesson.

Two hands, surprising in their strength, clamped hold of Turkey's right wrist. Then the Texan pivoted, carrying the trapped arm upwards and pulling on it in a certain manner. Much to the amazement of the onlookers, Turkey's feet left the ground and his body somersaulted through the air, passed over the Texan's shoulder and lit down, with a considerable raising of dust, flat on his back in the center of the street.

Having seen his brother in action against local boys, Coop did not expect his assistance would be needed against a small, insignificant man like the Texan. That he followed on Turkey's heels had been merely so he could lend a hand with the subsequent beating delivered to the rash stranger. Although unable to ascribe anything other than pure luck to the way the Texan threw his brother, Coop decided against too close action until the Texan had been rendered suitable for treatment. Pausing only long enough to slide the pool cue through his fingers until he gripped it at the thin end, Lanny moved forward after Coop. While Lanny figured Coop ought to be able to handle the Texan, he believed in being prepared.

While on a visit to Abilene, Coop had seen a French Creole *savate* fighter give a demonstration of foot-boxing and decided that the method possessed several advantages, including surprise, when used on an unexpecting opponent. So he practised, as best he could without competent instruction, the various kicking moves performed by the Frenchman. When in a fight, Coop tended to rely on his feet far more than his hands; a tactic which brought him some considerable success against the untutored youth of the region. Bracing him-

self, Coop launched a kick aimed at the Texan's groin.
Struck there, sheer agony would spoil the luck which
brought the Texan success in his first two encounters.

Unfortunately for Coop, to bring about the desired
result the kick must land. Crossing his wrists with the
right underneath, the Texan held them down so that
Coop's leg slipped into the X-shape they formed and
halted inches from its destination. Instantly the Texan
caught Coop's right trouser leg in his right hand and
pushed it away from him. Coop howled in surprise as he
felt himself losing his balance and fought to stay
upright. Held in such a manner, Coop could do nothing
against his assailant; a fact which struck the young man
with horrible impact. If Coop could do nothing, the
same did not apply to the Texan. Like a flash, he kicked
up with his right leg, driving it with sickening force into
the area on Coop which that worthy intended to kick on
the Texan.

Showing a masterly judgment of the situation, Lanny
came in from behind the Texan; having made a rapid
change of route when he saw that Coop failed to lay
their man low. Letting out a yell, Lanny whipped the
cue up over his head and sprang forward even as the
Texan completed Coop's discomfiture by kicking him.
The yell proved to be a serious error in tactics, for it
warned the Texan of further danger. Still retaining his
hold of Coop's pants leg, the Texan bent the upper part
of his body forward. He timed the move just right.
Down and around lashed the cue. It passed over the
Texan's body and thudded into Coop's ribs, serving,
along with the kick, to completely unbalance the agony-
filled young man and topple him over. At that moment
Lanny might have felt sympathy for his friend, but had
too many troubles of his own. Still bent forward, the
Texan whipped his right foot from where it landed on

Coop and drove it backwards under Lanny's striking arms to catch him full in the pit of the stomach. Breath rushed from Lanny's lungs under the impact of the kick and he reeled back, doubling over as his hands released his cue and clutched at the injured region.

Nor did Lanny's troubles end so lightly. Straightening up, the Texan heaved at the stricken Coop's leg and pitched him away. Still moving at top speed, the small man turned, caught the falling cue and slashed it down on to the back of Lanny's head. While the cue snapped in half, it packed enough punch to drop the man in a limp heap on the ground, where he lost all interest in the proceedings.

Snarling curses and shaking his head to clear the spinning in it caused by the Texan's blow, Gartree clung to the hitching-rail. He recovered sufficiently to see and understand what lay before him. Cold fear burst into Gartree, driving away the pain and nausea as he realised that in a very short time the Texan would be free to turn further attentions his way. Even as Coop toppled over and the cue whistled around to break on Lanny's head, Gartree decided to take a further hand in the game. Face contorted with rage, mingled with fear, Gartree reached for his gun. He saw the girl's head jerk around towards him and read the horror on it. Then she swung back to stare in the direction of the Texan.

Even though he had his back to Gartree, the Texan appeared to sense his danger. The instant the girl looked at him, although she never said a word, the Texan swung around to meet the fresh danger. One glance told him all he needed to know and he acted on his findings with the same speed which accompanied all his movements since taking a hand in the same. Lacking the time to leap forward and lay hands on Gartree, the Texan whipped back his arm and hurled the broken cue in a spinning line. Turning around and around in the air, the cue's end struck Gartree's right arm a hard smack. While the blow stung, it would not have had such a devastating effect if Gartree had not been making a very foolish mistake.

In drawing his gun, Gartree tried to follow the procedure practised by all the top fast men. His thumb closed around the hammer and began to draw it back as soom as his fingers gripped the Colt's butt. While this acted as an aid to speedy discharge when using a single-action weapon, which had to be cocked manually before it could fire, the move could only be performed safely if the action reached full cock *after* the barrel cleared leather and pointed away from the user's body.

Gartree lacked the necessary co-ordination and so cocked his Colt with its barrel still in leather. To make things worse, he committed the incredible folly of also squeezing the trigger while the gun still remained in the holster. Of course, nothing would have happened as long as his thumb stayed on the hammer.

On landing, the flying pool cue hurt Gartree enough to make him forget to take the basic precaution of holding back the hammer. He yelped in pain and relaxed his thumb's hold. Freed from restraint, the hammer snapped down and struck the copper head of the waiting percussion cap. Inside the gun, a tiny spurt of flame licked into and ignited the powder in the up-permost chamber of the cylinder. With a crack, the powder turned into a cloud of gas and hurled the bullet along the barrel, to emerge, rip through the bottom of the holster and down Gartree's leg. The young man let out a screech of agony and dropped, writhing and squealing, to the ground.

A shocked silence followed the sound and result of the shot, chopping off the excited comments aroused

by the Texan's remarkable efficiency in handling his
attackers. Every member of the crowd stared in stunned
amazement at the writhing, shrieking shape on the
ground. Not that Gartree continued to disturb the
silence for long. Pain and his cowardly nature soon
combined to tip him over into black unconsciousness.

So sudden and unexpected had been the Texan's
arrival and action that nobody in the crowd quite
understood what happened. All they knew for sure was
that Gavin Gartree lay wounded in the leg and his three
companions, who had terrorised the town for months,
sprawled on the street too concerned with their own
hurts to raise any further fuss. The entire incident could
be measured in seconds, almost too fast for the citizens
of Bainesville to follow. Lacking leadership, the townspeople stood and stared, unsure of what they ought to
do.

At this point Bainesville's town marshal arrived;
although it was doubtful if he possessed either the personality or ability to supply the leadership the crowd
needed. Thick set, bearded, slovenly dressed, Town
Marshal Gruber came lumbering along the street. Then
he skidded to a halt and his eyes took in the scene.

"What happened," he spat out, hardly able to drag
his horrified eyes away from the still shape of Gavin
Gartree.

"You mean to say you don't know," answered the
Texan. "You've been stood at the door of the jail ever
since this started."

"Don't hand me any lip, b——" Gruber began.

The words died away to nothing as the marshal suddenly became aware of a remarkable change which came
over the man before him. Suddenly the Texan ceased to
be small and insignificant. In some way he seemed to
have put on height and weight until he gave the im-

pression of towering over every man in the watching
crowd. Shocked by the inexplicable change, Gruber
stood very still and ran the tip of his tongue over lips
which felt strangely dry. Small the Texan might be in ac-
tual feet and inches, but he stood a man full-grown and
capable of backing any play he made. If Gruber tried
pushing the Texan, he knew he stood a better than fair
chance of winding up in water way over his head.
Gruber had never been a man to take long chances if he
could avoid them.

So, searching for a way out, one which would save his
face and keep him in a job which paid good wages for
the minimum of effort, Gruber turned his attention to
the more harmless-appearing strangers.

"All right!" he barked. "On your wagon and get the
hell out of town. We don't want your kind here causing
fuss and ruckus."

"*They* never caused any," the Texan put in.

Knowing how the average Kansas citizen regarded
members of the small religious sects which did not con-
form to the general line, Gruber felt sure that he could
rely on the crowd's backing while following his present
course.

"Nobody asked them to come, and if they
hadn't———"

"When I rode in, I didn't see any signs telling
strangers to keep out," the Texan answered. "Why
don't you pick on the right cause óf the fuss, Marshal?"

"Huh?"

"Get the right ones, those yahoos who started it."

While the two men spoke, the local doctor arrived.
Walking forward and ignoring the crowd, the doctor
dropped to one knee at Gartree's side and bent forward
to examine the wound. The Cooper brothers and Lanny
were recovering, but so far none of them felt up to

continuing the matter with the Texan. For the rest of those present, the local citizens stood back, watching and listening, but making no attempt to take part in the affair. The three travellers stood in a silent group and watched the Texan face the town marshal. Looking around him, Gruber saw no sign of help forthcoming from the crowd and wondered what his next move ought to be.

One way and another, Gruber could see endless trouble awaiting him, no matter how he handled the affair. Baines Gartree would expect that the man who crippled his son be arrested; even though the Texan acted to save his life and had not been responsible for young Gartree's lack of knowledge where guns were concerned. However, Gruber knew that he could not attempt the arrest without the backing of enough men to counter the Texan's objections to the act.

Obtaining the necessary assistance would be a problem. Slowly Gruber ran his eyes over the crowd, searching each face in an attempt to reading how its owner felt about the matter. What he saw raised little encouragement in his heart. He knew, without being told, that Gartree's bunch long since forfeited any sympathy or friendship around the town; and that, if anything, the crowd secretly approved of the Texan's actions in quelling the young trouble-causers. In general, Kansans disliked Texans—especially those, like the citizens of Bainesville, who received none of the financial benefits from the Texas trail herds which enriched the railway towns—but Gruber doubted if he could arouse the crowd on that score under the circumstances.

Not knowing what to do, Gruber showed enough sense to follow the only course left open to him and do nothing. In an attempt to hide his uncertainty in the matter, he turned from the Texan and looked to where the doctor had just finished a primary inspection of the wound.

"How is it, Doc?" he asked, trying to sound efficient.

"Bad. How the hell did you expect it to be?" snorted the doctor, who had few illusions about the marshal.

"Maybe I should———" growled Gruber, not sure just what he should do and leaving the blank in hope that the doctor supplied him with advice as to his next move.

"If you want to do anything, tell those three young fools to come help me carry Gartree home."

"Huh?" gulped Gruber, never the quickest of thinkers, making use of his favorite term when puzzled.

"Get the Coopers and Bulmer over here," explained the doctor savagely. "They helped get him into this state, so they can help tote him home. I might—only might—be able to save his leg if I hurry."

"Perhaps I could help," suggested the elder of the travellers, walking slowly towards the doctor.

"You," sneered Gruber, then shut his mouth as the doctor directed a cold scowl in his direction.

"Are you a doctor," asked the local medical man.

"I have some knowledge of medical matters."

"Then come and take a look."

Walking up, the bearded man knelt by the doctor's side and looked at the long tear in Gartree's flesh. Already the doctor had applied a tourniquet in an attempt to stop the bleeding, but the full horror of the wound showed plainly.

"Is there anything you can do," asked Gruber.

"That depends," answered the old man.

"On what," the doctor inquired. "You're not one of those faith healers, are you, mister?"

"We don't want any of that kind of rubbish here if you are," Gruber spat out. "This's a decent, church-going town and———"

For all the notice taken, the marshal might not have been speaking.

"I do not know what you mean by 'faith-healer', " the old man replied. "While I could mend this wound, I lack the equipment."

"If I've anything at my place———" the doctor began, wondering if he did the right thing.

"It is doubtful. Your wor—country is not far advanced medically."

"Mister," snapped the doctor. "I don't know where you come from, or how far advanced you figure you are. But you couldn't fix that leg so he'll walk on it without at best a bad limp."

"If I had———" the old man started.

"If you'd wings, you could fly out of here!" snarled Gruber. "And I———"

"Dry off!" ordered the doctor. "Just how would you start fixing the wound, stranger?"

"You have not the apparatus necessary," the old man answered sadly. "There is nothing I can do for so serious an injury."

"Reckon your old country's not much further advanced than our's then," the doctor commented. "Thanks for the offer. I'll get him home and do what I can." His eyes turned to where Gartree's friends managed to stand up. "Come over here and lend a hand with him."

While the trio felt that they ought to make a move of some kind against the Texan, each one realised that he might possibly be able to copper any bets they made. True the ease with which he handled them in the first place stemmed from their failing to appreciate his real potential. Now they knew and the knowledge left them uneasy. No longer did the Texan look small and insignificant and they welcomed the doctor's order as an excuse to avoid further tangling with the Texan.

Trying to appear reluctant, the three young men advanced and lifted Gartree. Profane warning of what would happen should they cause further damage to the injured limb crackled about the trio's ears as the doctor supervised them. With Gartree lifted and started along the street towards his home, the doctor paused and looked at the old stranger. Then, with a shrug, the doctor turned and walked away. When he came to think back on the incident, the doctor found himself wondering at why he felt such faith in the old man. For a moment he almost believed that the stranger possessed the means to heal young Gartree's limb; even though he knew this to be an impossibility. There had been an air about the bearded old man, something the doctor could not define or explain. "Of course," the doctor frequently mused when remembering the incident, "nothing on this earth could have repaired the damage Gartree's folly caused."

"What'll I tell Baines Gartree?" moaned Gruber, half to himself, as he watched the removal of the injured man.

"Why not tell him the truth," asked the Texan.

"The truth?"

"That his son tried to molest a girl in the street and got hurt trying to shoot me in the back."

"He hadn't——"

"Don't tell me that he was pulling that gun to swat flies," drawled the Texan sardonically. "Or that he wasn't laying hands on the young lady there against her will!"

"Shucks, young Gavin wouldn't've hurt her," objected the marshal. "He was only funning her along."

"Do you believe in fairies, too," growled the Texan.

Something in the small man's tone warned Gruber not to continue along that line in the matter. Taken any further, it would be tantamount to calling the Texan a liar; and Gruber knew what the consequences would be. So he swivelled his eyes in the direction of the travellers, watching the elder man join the other two.

"Damn it to hell!" he said pettishly. "If they hadn't come————"

"You've already said that," interrupted the Texan coldly.

"Us plain, church-going folks here in Bainesville don't go for having Mormons or their like coming here and stirring up trouble."

A low rumble of talk welled up among the crowd; not yet hostile, but likely to turn that way if given the right kind of inducement. Despite his small size, the Texan had been around enough and seen sufficient of life to be aware of how many Kansans—especially in the smaller towns—regarded Mormons in particular and the lesser religious sects in general. If the town marshal continued unchecked with his current line of talk, he might stir up the citizens. By playing on their desire to defend the honour of their church against unbelievers, he could start something serious. With that in mind, the Texan decided to declare his feeling on the matter.

"Understand one thing, all of you," he said quietly, his grey eyes raking the crowd in deadly emphasis to his words. "These folks came in peaceable and made no fuss. They'll leave the same way. Does anybody aim to try and stop them?"

Although every man in the crowd knew that the Texan had thrown down the gauntlet, not one of them intended to take up the challenge. Seeing no acceptance, the Texan turned and walked towards the girl. The grim lines left his face as he drew near, being replaced by a smile which transformed him once more into the small, pleasant-featured nonentity whose appearance so fooled Gartree's bunch.

"I'd like to thank you for yelling the warning, ma'am," he said. "I hadn't expected that jasper to be able to take a hand so soon."

"It was obvious that you were not aware of the danger," she replied. "And it is I who must thank you."

"Forget it, ma'am. Do you want anything here in town."

"No. I think not."

"If you want to buy supplies, nobody'll stop you."

After directing a glance in the elder man's direction, but not speaking, the girl shook her head. "We have all we need."

"We will continue our journey, there is nothing in this town that we seek," the old man went on. "Unless I could render assistance to the wounded man."

"Do you reckon you could do anything, sir?" the Texan asked. "If so, maybe I could talk the doctor into letting you try."

"Perhaps———" began the old man, then hesitated, looking at his two companions but not speaking.

"Sure," said the Texan, guessing at the cause of the other's hesitation. "That must have been a real bad wound. I didn't see it, but I've seen one caused in the same way."

"Perhaps my interference would cause complications," admitted the old man. "Your wor—country is not———"

Once again his words trailed off. He seemed uncertain of how to continue, like a guest waiting to make a complaint, but wishing to avoid offending his host.

"It is best that we continue our journey," the young man stated.

"Yes," agreed the elder. "We will leave this town and look for another, more suitable place."

"Which way're you going, sir," asked the Texan.

"To the—south."

"So am I. But I have to take my paint to the blacksmith's shop and have a shoe fixed first. If you care to wait, I'll ride along with you."

After directing a searching glance at the crowd and studying the marshal for a few seconds, the elder man shook his head. "No. It will be better for everybody if we leave now."

"If you're travelling far, you'd maybe best let the blacksmith look over your own team," the Texan suggested. "There's no other town for maybe two hundred miles down to the south."

"We had them attended to at the last town," the younger man answered. "We will be on our way."

The girl directed glances at her companions, without speaking to either. It almost seemed that she asked a question, yet not a word passed between the trio. At last she turned back to the Texan and smiled.

"Perhaps you can—catch up, is that the expression I want?—with us on the trail."

"Likely I will, ma'am," answered the Texan. "Allow me."

Stepping forward, he helped the girl up on to the wagon box, then stepped back and watched the two men mount. Although the girl smiled in the Texan's direction and raised her hand, none of the trio spoke as the wagon moved away.

Seeing that nothing more of note was likely to happen, the crowd began to disperse. Only rarely did anything exciting occur to break the even, uneventful flow of their lives and the happenings of that day would provide the citizens with conversation and speculation for months to come.

The local blacksmith joined the Texan as his fellow citizens broke up to go about their interrupted affairs.

"I'm sorry I wasn't at my place when you came in earlier, friend," he said. "This's my day for tending to the Wells Fargo stock."

"I needed a haircut and it gave me time to have one."

"If you'll fetch your horse along now, I'll tend to it."

"Why sure," agreed the Texan, throwing a glance at the departing wagon.

"They're a strange bunch," remarked the blacksmith. "But that was a pretty gal."

"It sure was," the Texan replied, and went to collect his waiting paint.

CHAPTER THREE

Baines Gartree's Hired Man

"Your boy will never walk again."

Halting in the pacing he had been doing across the width of the well-furnished sitting-room, Baines Gartree stared at the doctor and let the words sink into his numbed head. Although the gravity on the doctor's face should have warned Gartree, the politician had fought off the thought and hoped for the best. Now he knew the truth.

Big, fashionably dressed in Eastern style, slightly bald and wearing spectacles, Gartree carried himself with an air of pompous superiority. For once the air departed. His mouth normally tight and unsmiling—he invariably announced that, with the country in its present state, it was no time for levity; a profound statement which did him an enormous amount of good among the sober citizens of the Cyclone State—shrank to a mere slit; and a dull red color crept into his normally sallow cheeks.

"You're sure, Doctor?" he gritted.

"Well, I might not be one of those fancy big-city surgeons," the doctor replied coldly; thinking that in all the time they had known each other, Gartree never once addressed him by name or even as 'Doc'. "But I've seen enough gun-shot wounds to know a mite about them."

"And there's nothing more can be done?"

"Not that I know of."

"Nothing, not even if we sent Gavin back east?"

"I try to keep up with the latest developments there. If there was anything anyplace that could help, I'd suggest it. That old feller with the wagon offered to do something. Maybe he could."

"Is he a qualified doctor?"

"Didn't say," admitted the doctor.

"Most likely he's a faith-healer!" snorted Gartree. "One of those lousy 'Pray-with-me-and-get-the-right-side-of-our-God-and-you'll-be-cured' bigots."

Eyeing Gartree, the doctor wondered what had happened to the stand the politician took in the State Legislature on the subject of religious tolerance; a campaign which earned him the votes of a large Jewish community. Being a man who believed in fair play at all times, not only when it offered political advantage, the doctor tried to set the record straight.

"Feller never made any such claims to me. He could be a doctor of some kind."

"I don't want a doctor of 'some kind' round my son!" Gartree spat out. "Especially when it was through his slut that my son got shot."

Although the doctor did not agree with Gartree's version of how the young man came to be injured, he had to live in Bainesville and remembered what happened to other people who crossed the "liberal" politician. So he kept his opinions to himself. He still felt curious at his attitude in regard to the old man as a possibility in the recovery of young Gartree. While the doctor had no faith in the kind of medicine showman who travelled the West peddling "miraculous" cures to the unwary, nothing he saw about the strangers hinted that they belonged to that class of drifter. Giving a shrug, the doctor dismissed the thoughts. Certain as he had been earlier, nothing seen on closer examination led him to believe Gavin Gartree's limb could be healed and made fit to use.

"There's no more I can do for the time being," he said. "He's sleeping and I've given him laudanum to help deaden the pain. If he recovers, send for me. If not, I'll be in this evening to see him."

"Can't you stay here?" asked Gartree.

"I've other patients to visit."

Just as Gartree opened his mouth to damn the interests of the other patients, he realised that such would be out of character with the image he showed the public. He contented himself with scowling at the doctor for a moment, then nodded.

"All right, Doctor. Thank you, I know you've done your best."

Clearly Gartree wanted the visit to end and the doctor had no desire to prolong it. Collecting his hat and bag from the small table by the room's main door, the doctor left. After a couple of minutes' pacing, Gartree appeared to reach a decision. Two other doors led into the sitting-room and he strode to the one on the left. Jerking open the door, he looked through it.

"Come in!" he ordered.

Looking like a puppy expecting a whipping for wetting on the carpet, Marshal Gruber slouched into the room. A second man followed, but he walked with an air of easy familiarity and equality which Gartree always found irritating and never more so than at that moment. Without showing the slightest interest in the scowl Gartree directed at him, the second man went to the table in the center of the room and helped himself to a cigar from the box and then poured out a drink from the cut glass decanter.

"Why the hell didn't you arrest the man who assaulted my boy, Marshal," Gartree snarled, taking out his objections to the second man's actions upon the safer target offered by Gruber.

Although he showed some discomfort at the question, Gruber failed to make any answer for some seconds. Once clear of the Texan's presence, the marshal found himself unable to put an adequate reason to his failing to quell such a small, insignificant person. In the past Gruber had met with some success in handling local cowhands of far more imposing appearance than the Texan, and could not decide just how he came to fail.

"I thought the other two would jump me," he said lamely, making the only excuse which came to a slow-working mind.

A low guffaw of disbelief sounded from the second man and Gartree scowled viciously at the marshal. Word had already reached Gartree, brought by a man eager to curry the politician's favor, and he possessed a pretty fair idea of what happened on Cresset Street. Conveniently overlooking his son's part in starting the affair, Gartree knew only that Gavin received a serious wound at the hands of a Texan. If anything, the Texan's place of origin increased Gartree's hatred. Like most of his kind, Gartree had a bigoted hatred of anybody who failed to blindly follow his beliefs; and knew that very few sons of the Lone Star State accepted or subscribed to his ideals. Gartree wanted revenge on the man responsible and already started to plan means of taking it.

"What do you aim to do about the man, Gruber?" he demanded.

"You don't figure he can do anything, now do you?" sneered the other man.

If Gruber resented the words, he managed to conceal

his feelings. Unlike his predecessor—who Gartree caused to be discharged from office after the man handed a cheap young thief a beating for robbing an old woman—Gruber was no fighting man. The tall, lean man in the town suit, but wearing a low-hanging Adams Navy revolver in a fighting rig, could claim to being just that. In fact he drew good pay for his ability in the fighting line; his name was Jason Latter and his trade, professional killer.

Ignoring Latter's comment, Gartree faced the marshal and held the lawman's eyes with his own. "I want that Texan arrested on a charge of attempted murder, Gruber."

"How about it, John Law?" grinned Latter. "You reckon you can take him?"

Gruber did not reply, but ran his tongue tip across his lips.

"If you need a deputy to help," Gartree continued, "I reckon that Mr. Latter will go along."

"I'll go, but not with him alongside me," Latter put in. "That Texan won't come in walking, and John Law there'd be as much use as an udder on a bull if it comes to a shoot-out."

"Marshal Gruber will deputise you," Gartree insisted, wanting to try to keep an air of legality about the affair.

"He don't need," sniffed the killer. "And when I take a badge, it won't be as his, or anybody else's, deputy. If you want that Texan, say the word and I'll go get him for you."

"Well, I suppose that you can use your Constitutional rights and make a citizen's arrest," admitted Gartree. "If you feel you can't take a badge, but must do your duty, that is the only way."

"Yeah," agreed Latter. "That's the only way. I'll go along and take in that Texan. How'd you want him taken?"

"Huh?" grunted Gartree.

"Do you want him walking, or slung across his saddle?" Latter inquired. "It all comes the same to me, but you're paying for it."

"You know how I feel about such things," Gartree replied, ignoring the last part of his hired man's speech. "I always say that a lawman should use the minimum amount of force possible when making an arrest."

"That's what you always say," Latter grinned. "I'll go tend to him. Mind what we was talking about this morning. I'd admire to be marshal of an up-and-coming town like this."

While speaking, the killer removed his jacket and hung it over the back of a chair. He acted with complete confidence, more like a social equal than an employee—and an undesirable employee at that. After loosening the Adams in its holster, Latter directed a contemptuous leer at the marshal, nodded cheerfully to Gartree and walked from the room.

Two pairs of hate-filled eyes followed the killer until the door closed behind him, and neither of the remaining men spoke for several seconds. Gartree spent the time in rapid thought, making plans and wondering how he might bring them to a successful conclusion.

"Latter was asking me this morning to use my influence and have him appointed town marshal in your place," he finally told Gruber.

"Folks wouldn't want a hired killer like him running the law," scoffed Gruber, then thought what losing his post would mean to him. "Would they?"

"You know the ingratitude of the public," Gartree answered. "They're so fickle that they forget all the good things you've done if they think you've failed them.''

''I don't follow you,'' Gruber stated, knowing he had done little good while in office.

''If Latter arrests the Texan, the citizens are going to start asking why you didn't do it. The ones who are discontented with you will start saying we need a new marshal, then begin asking why they elected you in the first place.''

Gruber could well imagine a number of people asking that question and coming up with the wrong answers from his point of view. ''What should I do?'' he moaned.

''It's not for me to tell you how to do your duty, Marshal,'' Gartree replied, picking out each word with care and pausing for emphasis before continuing, ''but if I was in your place, I'd take serious exception to an outsider attempting to make a citizen's arrest in my town.''

''You mean I should stop him?''

''*That* is up to you.''

''I thought he worked for you,'' said Gruber in a puzzled tone, realising what the stopping might entail.

''*Him?*'' snorted Gartree. ''He doesn't work for me. Came to ask my assistance in obtaining justice for a cousin who's been wrongly jailed. What would I need with the services of a man like him?''

''Nothing, I should reckon,'' Gruber answered. ''Won't he be riled if I cut in, though?''

''He might be—if you give him the chance.''

''You mean I should———?''

Gartree was too old a hand at the political game to be caught in making a definite statement which might be used against him.

''I mean nothing,'' he stated firmly. ''All I say is there are times when a duly-appointed officer of the law must use force to oppose force, and take firm measures to keep the peace.'' Seeing the marshal wavering, he continued, "I'll back you in any action you find it necessary to take.''

A thoughtful gleam came into Gruber's eyes at the last words. Although not a particularly intelligent man, he knew exactly what Gartree meant; and yet felt puzzled. For some reason or other, the politician did not want either Latter or the Texan alive at the end of the affair. While understanding Gartree's feelings towards the Texan, Gruber failed to see why the other wanted the hired killer dead.

Although not willing to disclose it, Gartree possessed an excellent reason for wanting Latter out of his life. During a recent campaign, it had become necessary to remove a too-popular opponent. While Gartree had arranged such things before, he never met the hired killer personally and dealt always through a second party. In some way or other Latter discovered that Gartree was behind the man who hired him. Presenting him to the politician, Latter announced his intention of taking full-time employment with Gartree—not a desirable arrangement for a man who drew many votes through peaching a policy of non-violence and tolerance. With Latter able to prove his statement, dismissing him was out of the question, as was refusing his suggestion. At last Gartree saw a way of removing the menace to his career—if only Gruber possessed the guts to do it.

Whichever way the affair went, Gartree stood to gain. If the Texan proved lucky enough to kill Latter, all well and good. More likely the shooting would go the other way; after all, Latter earned his living by winning gun fights. In that case, fear of losing an easy way of earning his keep might give Gruber the necessary courage to finish Latter off. Having a low, if accurate, opinion of the marshal's intelligence, Gartree figured he had nothing to fear from Gruber after the shooting. Gruber lacked the brains and reasoning power to try Latter's tricks, or attempt to cash in on his knowledge.

"I reckon I'd best go tend to it, Mr. Gartree," the marshal said, after some thought which got him nowhere.

"Good luck, Marshal," Gartree replied. "And don't forget that I'm behind you all the way."

Showing more geniality than the marshal could remember on previous meetings, Gartree ushered Gruber into the main hall and to the front door. After seeing the man out, Gartree turned, his face losing its friendly "I'll-support-you-through-thick-and-thin" expression. He turned and crossed the hall, climbed the stairs and entered his son's room. Halting just inside the door, Gartree looked across the darkened room to the still shape on the bed. Cold fury grew in the politician as his eyes went down to the raised blankets over the injured limb.

Give him his due, while an arrant snob, an opportunist, bigot and hypocrite, Gartree loved his son. Secretly he knew that his own actions brought about Gavin's injury. He had heard stories of his son's behavior around town and, although he openly declared it to be no more than high spirits, knew just how viciously Gavin acted. Knowing that his lack of control lay at the back of the incident hurt and Gartree wanted to swing the blame anywhere but on himself. Everyone connected with the incident must suffer. Already he had sent Latter to kill the Texan, but that was not enough. The people whose presence in Bainesville led to his son being crippled must also pay. Staring down at his son, Gartree tried to decide how he should go about taking his revenge on the travellers.

The door opened behind Gartree and he turned to find his butler entering.

"Mr. Gavin's friends are downstairs in the kitchen, sir," the butler said.

Opening his mouth to order them sent away, Gartree stopped with the words unsaid. Ideas flashed into his head, clicking into place and meeting with his approval. Instead of replying, he threw another glance at his son and walked from the room. Entering the kitchen, he found the Coopers and Lanny Bulmer standing at the table and helping themselves to coffee. If they felt any embarrassment, none of them showed it.

"How's Gav?" asked Turkey.

"Crippled for life!" Gartree gritted out. "Why didn't you three do something to stop it?"

"We for sure tried," Lanny answered. "Only that Texan, he wouldn't let us."

"He sure wouldn't," agreed Coop.

"Damn it to hell! There were three of you against him."

"Four, mister," Turkey corrected coldly. "Only your son didn't show worth shucks when the fuss started."

Gartree's eyes went to Turkey's face, fury glowing in them. Studying the young man, the politician read insolence and danger in the return stare. Ever since their first meeting, Turkey worried Gartree. The young man dearly wanted to gain the coveted title of killer and might not be choosey how he took the first step towards that end. One wrong word or action and Turkey, already smarting under the knowledge that he failed when put to the test, might strike blindly. So Gartree overlooked the other's attitude, although it hardened his resolve, and went on with the plan formulated on the way downstairs.

"What do you intend to do about Gavin?" he asked. "I thought *men* like you would want to get evens for a friend."

While Gartree saw that his emphasis on the word 'men' struck the right note, the trio failed to show any great enthusiasm.

"You reckon we should ought to take out after that Texan again?" asked Coop.

"No. He's been taken care of—I mean, the marshal's gone to arrest him."

The whoops of laughter which followed Gartree's words did not sound complimentary to Marshal Gruber.

"Him? Ole Tin Star?" scoffed Coop. "Why he couldn't arrest a one-armed, one-legged, blind, deaf and white-haired Digger Injun without a posse to back him up."

"Happen that lil Texas boy can shoot like he fist-fights," Lanny went on, "this here town's going to come shy a marshal real sudden."

"Forget the Texan, he's being dealt with," Gartree growled. "It's the other bunch, that girl who egged Gavin on, and her menfolks that I'm thinking about."

"And you want for us to go after them?" asked Turkey.

"Why not? Gavin was a good friend to you."

"You want for us to go out after them folks and rough-handle them some?" Turkey went on, a calculating glint in his eyes.

"I didn't say that. I'm leaving it to you *men* whether you let a bunch of strangers come into your town and get a good friend shot by their hired killer."

"Was it my son, I'd come along and make sure it got done right."

For a long time Gartree did not reply to Cooper's words. He used the silence to think fast and reached certain conclusions. While he did not intend, in the first place, to take any active part in avenging his son, he decided it might be to his advantage to go along. When the shooting happened, he should be out of town and in a position later to deny all knowledge of why Latter went after the Texan. He also felt a desire to see the travellers suffer, that might ease the nagging guilt which filled him.

"Get the horses, I'll come with you," he said and read surprise on the three young faces. "You're right, Gavin's my son and I should be there."

"They've a good two hours start," Coop commented. "But happen we push the hosses, we ought to catch up with them easy enough."

"And close to town," Turkey growled. "Like hell we do. We'll follow those pilgrims until nightfall. Even if they don't know the country, they'll have reached Tuliptree Springs just afore dark and they'll make camp there, or I don't know their kind. That's where we'll jump them—well clear of town."

Although the arrangement did not fit into Gartree's plans, he could see the two young men agreed to it. So he raised no arguments, merely changing the details of his first idea to fit the new circumstances.

"That's the best idea," he said. "Let's make a start."

On leaving the room Gartree found his butler waiting. The Negro fetched out his employer's gunbelt as requested and looked the politician over with expressionless eyes.

"Will you-all be gone long, sir?"

"I may be away all night."

"Yes, sir," said the butler, his eyes drifting to the stairs.

"I know I can rely on you to see to Mister Gavin for me," Gartree said, guessing at the other's thoughts. "And my business is urgent."

"Yes, sir."

"I want to go after those people and tell them that I don't hold any grudge against them for what happened to Gavin."

"That sure is the Christian way, sir."

Throwing a long, searching glance at the butler, in an attempt to see if veiled sarcasm lay behind the comment, Gartree read nothing in the impassive black face. He felt that he had achieved his object and possessed a witness to testify to the purity of his intentions in visiting the travellers. After ordering that his son was not to be left unattended, Gartree left the house.

The three young men had known that their free-meal-and-drink times were over and only called at the house in the hope of picking up a grub-stake—a thing Coop, cynical by nature, claimed to be as likely as catching sun-stroke in the middle of a blizzard. So their horses stood saddled and waiting outside the rear of the Gartree house. That only left Gartree to collect a horse, saddle it and mount. He did so in a fair time, considering that he usually left such details to a servant, and the party turned their horses in the direction of the southern trail.

Before they had gone a hundred yards, the four men heard the crackle of shots from the poorer section of town. First came the flat barking of revolvers; three shots in all, one heavy and a lighter crack very close together followed by a second heavy crack. Then they heard a yell, too distant for them to understand the words, echoed by the deep boom of a shotgun and an

instant later the deep bark of the revolver jarred the air
again. Silence followed for a few seconds before shouts
rose from Cresset Street.

"Sounds like the Texan's been taken care of,"
Turkey commented, glancing at Gartree as he spoke.

"Tolerable amount of shooting to take care of just
one man though," Coop went on.

Gartree did not reply, seeing no point in mentioning
that he hoped more than one man died. If it came to a
point, he hoped that at least three men went under; for
he had no desire to have Gruber around knowing what
he did. While the marshal might lack the brains to utilise
his knowledge, he could fall into the hands of somebody
who could. So, on the whole, Gartree preferred that
Gruber died doing his "duty" rather than lived as a
menace to a promising political career.

Suddenly Gartree became aware of a restlessness
among his young companions. All sat looking in the
direction of the shooting and worry-lines creased their
faces. Turkey turned and looked at Gartree.

"That hired gun of your'n packed an Adams, didn't
he?"

"If you mean Mr. Latter, he's nothing——" Gartree began, but the young man ignored him.

"And the Texan toted a brace of Army Colts,"
Turkey continued.

"Man don't miss with a scatter too often," Lanny
commented.

"Not often," agreed Coop. "You wanting to stay
and see what happened, Mr. Gartree?"

"No. The marshal can handle things. We'll go after
those pilgrims and teach them a lesson they'll never
forget."

CHAPTER FOUR

Bainesville's Blacksmith Shows Caution

"You sure live right, friend," Clint Morley, the blacksmith, told the small Texan as they walked along the main street in the direction of his forge. "If you hadn't turned when you did———" He shook his head before continuing. "I'm not saying that young Gartree would have shot you in the back; but a man'd need to be real brave—or plumb foolish—to rely on it."

"You could be right at that," admitted the Texan. "It's lucky for me that that girl yelled for me to watch him."

"She yelled?"

"Sure. Why else do you think I'd've known to turn?"

A puzzled frown crossed the burly blacksmith's open, cheery face. Although he had not been close enough to take part in the fracas, he approached during its latter stages and could not remember hearing the girl shout any warning. Of course, he had been fully absorbed in studying the Texan's unusual, highly effective, fighting techniques; but he doubted if he would miss such an important detail as the girl's participation by warning the Texan of his danger.

Knowing better than appear to doubt the Texan's word, Morley swung the conversation away from that aspect of the affair and decided that he should hand out a warning.

"Gartree's father's not going to forget or forgive you for what happened to his boy."

"Would that be Baines Gartree, the politician?"

"The very same."

"He's a right big man in your State Legislature, they do tell. Got his eyes set on the Governor's chair, or a seat in the U.S. Congress."

"Yeah," grunted Morley, surprised that his companion should be so well informed about Kansas politics.

"Could even get one or the other."

"He keeps saying out loud all the time that he doesn't want either."

"I never saw the politician who didn't—when he wanted to be elected for something or other."

Morley directed a searching glance at the Texan, wondering where such an insignificant young man met politicians—or learned to speak with such cynical certainty on the subject of their behavior. More than ever, the blacksmith came to wonder about the young man by his side, trying to decide who he might be. Whoever he was, that small Texan did not belong to the ordinary herd, no matter how he looked, or Morley sadly missed his guess.

"Sounds like you know politicians," the blacksmith grinned.

"I've met some," admitted the Texan. "They're just like people."

"Same being true, I'd put me some miles between me and Bainesville, was I you."

"Not until my paint's ready to ride."

"Which's why you're coming with me. But when it's done, I'd ride fast until I joined up with a Texas outfit. Baines Gartree won't take kind to you crippling his son for no reason—and that's how he'll look at it, with never a thought to why you did what you did."

"He's a man of peace, they do tell me," the Texan commented dryly.

"A dove's the bird of peace, but they fight like hell," answered Morley. "What I've said still goes."

"I wasn't fixing to set up home here, the winters're too cold," the Texan drawled. "Got to meet some of my *amigos* down in the Nations at Bent's Ford by the end of the week. You don't reckon that Gartree'd put the law on to me, do you?"

"It's possible."

"There were plenty of witnesses saw why I did it."

"Sure."

"Only you don't think they'd admit I acted the only way I could?"

"Let's say they might find trouble remembering just what did happen."

"Because I'm a Texan?"

"No," answered Morley. "We're too far East to see enough of you to form any opinions. But they have to go on living here after you've left; and things seem to go all unlucky for people Baines Gartree doesn't like."

"Do you reckon he'll make fuss for you because you've helped me leave town?" asked the Texan. "I'd not get too far without the shoe being fixed."

"I reckon not," stated Morley with quiet conviction. "Got a few good friends hereabouts, they represent a whole solid chunk of votes. Nope, I don't think Baines Gartree'll chance making fuss for me."

By that time, the two men had left Cresset Street and passed between the buildings of the poorer side of town. The blacksmith's forge stood at the rear of the houses, clear of them. While approaching, the Texan studied the pay-out of Morley's business premises. Under a large, open-fronted building, a fire glowed redly in the fur-

nace. Two black workers made horseshoe nails with
speed and precision on the anvil. Everything about the
place showed a neat orderliness which impressed the
Texan. A man could safely leave his horse—more than a
means of transport, being a necessity of life to a
Texan—in the care of the Bainesville blacksmith; or the
appearance of his place lied badly.

For his part, Morley studied the Texan and the big
paint stallion with equal interest. The horse appeared to
be in first-class condition, its coat, rich deer-red
splashed with white, glowed in health; head carried
proudly high, with bright eyes and clean, flaring
nostrils. There was a man's mount, the kind of animal
anybody would be proud to own. Not that just anybody
could handle such a spirited beast. Being a shrewd judge
of a horse's nature, Morley knew instinctively that the
paint needed firm, capable handling.

Morley's eyes went to the small Texan, realising the
other must be a better than fair horseman to handle the
paint with such confidence. Under the strict code of
the range country Morley could not ask the obvious
question. Instead he glanced back in the hope of seeing
what brand the paint carried, but was on the wrong side
to read what might be a clue to his companion's identity.

"If you'll get him off-saddled and ready, we'll make
a start," Morley suggested as they arrived at the front of
the forge. "You'll be wanting a new shoe for him, I
reckon."

"Sure," the Texan agreed. "But make it of 'old stuff'
will you, please?"

Once again Morley directed a glance at the Texan and
a broad grin came to his lips. The blacksmith usually
asked a new customer what kind of materials he required to be used in shoeing his horse, and based his
judgment on the answer. Even without being asked, the

Texan gave the correct answer. The mention of "old stuff" came out too naturally to be a chance-learned term slipped in to impress the blacksmith with non-existent knowledge. Morley felt sure that the Texan would never try to impress anybody, and used the term knowing full well what it meant.

Horseshoes were made from either new bar iron, or old shoes moulded afresh and turned into shape. While new iron produced a satisfactory shoe in skilled hands, the hammering and heating necessary to refashion "old stuff" tempered it afresh and gave it an added tough-ness.

Knowing that the Texan understood the extra lasting qualities given by shoes made of "old stuff," Morley respected him all the more and prepared to give him the best possible workmanship.

Laying aside his hammer, the taller of the Negro strikers walked towards his boss and nodded to where the Texan turned to start removing the paint's saddle.

"I sure hopes that Texas gennel-man's a-going to be around while we works on his hoss, Mr. Clint."

"You scared of it, Bill?" grinned Morley.

"No, sah. It's only that I has to take my honey-chile to a dance tonight and I sure don't look my best with hoss-shoes sticking in my face."

Seeing that his striker's view on the paint's nature coincided with his own, Morley laughed and assured the man that the horse's owner intended to stick around during the shoeing. Morley did not regard his striker's caution as cowardice, but merely an extension of his own belief that the paint would not take kindly to having strangers handle it.

"Go get some heat under that fire, Bill," Morley ordered. "Ez, pick out a mould. We've got a hoss to shoe."

"Something told me you-all aimed to say that,

boss,'' the second striker replied, rolling his eyes as he studied the big paint. "Ah can't start my vacation right now, can I?''

"Danged if I don't think you're scared too," chuckled Morley.

"I ain't no more scared than you is, Mr. Clint," objected Ez.

"Don't know why I hire a feller that scared," countered the blacksmith. "I want one of *our* moulds."

The words told the strikers all they needed to know. It was Morley's custom to keep two stocks of moulds—used horseshoes prepared ready to be redrawn—those made by other smiths and left during shoeing, and his own stock. He always used his own material, tempered to the best of his ability in the first place, when shoeing the horse of a man he admired.

Working with smooth efficiency, the Texan stripped off his paint's saddle. He handled the forty-five pound range rig and its attachments without any observable difficulty, carrying it to the inverted V-shaped burro erected for customers' use. No man who knew anything about saddlery ever set down his rig on its skirts, and only laid it on its side when not in use if forced by necessity. Whenever possible a cowhand, depending more than most people on his saddle—without which he could not work and earn a living—preferred to rest it on a burro when not in use.

With his saddle cared for, the Texan took his horse first to the water trough and allowed it to drink, then led it to where the blacksmith stood waiting. Morley, donning his heavy leather apron, managed for the first time to see the paint's brand. Although he did not live in Texas, Morley knew who used the letters "O" and "D", so close together that they touched edges, to identify his stock. It was a well-known, famous even, brand; one with which a man associated

certain often-heard names. In fact, one name particularly came to mind when thinking of the OD Connected ranch in Texas; but that small, insignificant man
could not be the person Morley thought of no matter
how efficient he might act.

Putting his thoughts aside, Morley advanced toward
the horse. While he moved confidently, he kept a wary
eye on the horse and knew it watched him with the same
care. Left to himself, Morley would have stayed clear of
the horse, or taken measures to secure it. With the
Texan standing at the horse's head, he figured he need
have no fear. There were a number of ways in which the
horse could be controlled during shoeing. It might be
placed in a tight stall and prevented from turning on the
smith; or a twitch, a two foot six inch long, one and a
half inch diameter wooden pole with a leather running
loop at one end, could be attached to the upper lip as an
inducement to obey. With many men, Morley would
have demanded one or the other while working on such
a big, potentially dangerous animal. It said much for his
faith in the small man that he prepared to start the
shoeing while the other merely stood at the horse's
head. Reins gripped in strong hands, the Texan still
relied more on his voice to control his mount.

"Easy now, damn you to hell," said the Texan
gently, his tone belying the curse. "Just you stand easy
and let the nice Yankee gentleman fix up your foot, you
prick-eared, pig-eyed, roman-nosed, ewe-necked,
roach-backed, cow-hocked, off-colored slob of per-
versity. You kick him and I'll shoot you for hound-
dawg meat comes us getting back home. See if I don't."

Evidently the horse had become accustomed to its
owner's gentle-voiced slanders and accepted his master-
ship without question. Moving slowly, but without any
hint of concern, Morley took up his position and raised
the left rear leg for examination. The first thing to strike

him was something not often seen on horses of the period. Like the rest of the animal, the hoof showed signs of care and attention—but something more too.

"I had him cold-shod a couple of days out of Newton," the Texan remarked, never relaxing his hold of the reins. "Aimed to get it changed while I was there, but things kept coming up."

"I'll bet they did," grinned Morley; having seen Texas cowhands in the town after their drives paid off, he felt he could guess at the kind of things which prevented the other from attending to a minor detail. Then something else struck him. "This's a mighty good fit for a cold shoe."

"The man who did it for me learned how in the War. He handled all the shoeing for my company and did it real good. Had to. A man could get caught too easy if his horse went lame under him through losing a shoe. And, way I heard it, you Yankees didn't feed even officers too well."

Morley realised that the Texan paid him a compliment by speaking in such a manner. Peace at the Appomattox Court House did not bring an end to the hatreds of the Civil War and a Texan only joked that way with a Union supporter if he respected the other. The way the Texan spoke of 'my company' struck Morley as significant, for he used the term as if he commanded the company. Yet he could not have been more than seventeen or eighteen years old during the final years of the War. Of course, family influence put very young men in command of companies, especially in the Army of the Confederate States. Maybe the Texan had been one of that class; his easy drawl carried the undertones of an educated man.

Thinking of Texas-born Confederate cavalry leaders brought a name to Morley's mind, but he could hardly

credit his small customer with being the man he thought
of. And yet——

"A 'good-enough' doesn't often fit this well, no
matter how good the man who puts it on," he
remarked, wondering how he might satisfy his curiosity.

Every trail drive carried a keg of horseshoes of
assorted sizes in its bed-wagon, to be used as replace-
ments during the long journey north. While they served
their purpose, such shoes, called 'good-enoughs', rarely
formed a really good fit.

"I had a set made up for the paint before we left
home and toted them along. It's better than keep going
into the barrel."

"Reckon it is," Morley agreed. "You must've had a
mighty obliging trail boss."

"There's some who wouldn't say so," smiled the
Texan.

Applying the jaws of the pincers, Morley levered and
drew off the old shoe with a smooth, deft pull. With his
way to the hoof clear, he took up his sixteen inch long
rasp and began the delicate business of levelling the
bearing surface of the foot. He stopped talking, and
quit trying to decide his customer's identity, concentrating on his work. Carefully he rasped away such
of the hoof's horn as had grown since the last shoeing,
ensuring that he maintained the comparative level of the
heel and toe. While working, however, in the final
stages he could not help mentioning something noticed
earlier and which still interested him.

"You haven't had the horn or frog pared," he said;
wondering if it be an oversight, or if, by some miracle,
he had at last found somebody who subscribed to one of
his own pet theories.

"And I don't want them pared," the Texan replied
with the air of one prepared to take a firm stand on a

hotly-debated and highly controversial point.

"Don't, huh?"

"No. Way I see it, paring makes the horn brittle and ruins the frog. It's near as bad as dumping the toe."

The Texan spoke defensively, conscious of committing what, in the early 1870's, amounted to blacksmithing heresy.

While "dumping," cutting down the front wall of the foot instead of rasping away the surplus from the bearing surface to shorten the toe, was a serious fault in every horseman's eyes, most people swore by paring down the horny sole of the hoof and the frog. To do this, the smith cut away the thick, hard protective outer horn in the belief that it was detrimental to the elasticity of the foot. The exposed layer of soft horn soon became dry and brittle and the removal of the frog's excess growth—done in the erroneous belief that the frog was a delicate organ to be protected from injury by preventing its contact with the ground—stopped it performing its natural function of absorbing the concussion caused by the foot striking the ground when in motion.

"Packing the hoof with cow-dropping and clay soon cools it down after it's been pared," Morley commented.

"And makes it more brittle," argued the Texan. "Even after cooling, there comes a time when the foot gets so sore you have to turn the horse out to range graze on soft going until it settles again."

"Mind if I shake your hand when I've finished here?"

"Why?"

"You're the first I've met who goes along with me on this paring business. Most folks think the work's not properly done unless the sole's pared down until it'll spring under the thumb. Just don't listen to reason—except here in Bainesville."

"Why here?"

"I'm the only smith in maybe a hundred and fifty miles. Folks'd rather have it done my way, than travel that far every time a horse throws a shoe."

With that, the blacksmith pulled away a couple of flakes of horn which had worn loose and tripped out a few ragged bits of the frog, but did no more trimming in that area. Satisfied that he had levelled the foot correctly, Morley lowered the horse's leg and went over to where his strikers waited to make the shoe.

Standing at his horse's head, the Texan watched the next stage of the work; fascinated as always by the degree of skill such men showed when producing a shoe.

After checking that it had been heated enough, Morley removed the mould—an old horseshoe bent double and with half another wedged into the fold—which Bill had placed into the forge's glowing flames. At the anvil, the strikers beat the mould into a single length, then, with Morley manipulating it in his shoeing tongs, turned it into the shape of a shoe the size of the one removed from the paint.

A further heating came when the shoe was shaped and Morley carried the glowing iron forward. Taking up the paint's hoof once more, he held the shoe in place just long enough to sear the bearing surface until it turned brown. The color enabled him to check the shoe's fit and ensure that, being on the hind foot, it set back a little from the front of the toe so as to lessen the chance of injury should the horse over-reach—kick a foreleg with a hind—while galloping.

With the fit of the shoe to his satisfaction—such being Morley's skill that it needed only one minor adjustment in shape—he cooled it down and gave it a finishing polish with his file. On returning to the paint, he began to secure the shoe. Beginning at the toe, using sound, feel and experience, he drove in nail after nail.

Each nail went home at an angle which brought its tip
through the wall just high enough to give a secure hold.
On emerging, the projecting point was gripped in the
claw of the hammer and twisted off with a deft motion;
a precaution taken to save the smith's leg from being
torn open should the horse kick him. By pressing the
closed jaws of the pincers firmly upwards against the
broken end of the nail, repeated blows on its head with
the hammer caused a small portion of the shank to bend
over. Known as a clench, the bent-over piece was flat-
tened to the side of the wall as a further aid to holding
on the shoe. After a quick rasping down of any small
projections, Morley fitted the clips into place. Then he
set down the hoof and looked at the Texan.

"How'll it do for you?" he asked.

Although the Texan knew that the work would be
satisfactory, he did what he knew Morley expected of
him. Leaving the horse's head, he walked back and bent
to examine the shoe. Everything was just as he knew it
would be; the clenches flat, broad, neither too high nor
too low and no nail driven into the hole left by the
previous shoeing.

"I reckon it won't come off as I'm walking out of the
gate," he remarked, with a grin that belied the comment.

"Happen it does," Morley answered. "I'll put it on
free and without you holding the horse."

Neither man had given any thought to the passage of
time, nor to the events on Cresset Street which preceded
the Texan's visit to the forge. Even as Morley made
what he knew to be a safe promise, he saw something
which recalled his previous anxiety for his customer's
welfare.

CHAPTER FIVE

A Killer Stalks His Prey

After leaving the house, Jason Latter did not rush off wildly to begin his assignment. Unlike his employer, Latter had not heard the citizen's story of the incident and did not know where he might find his prey. However, he had seen enough of cowhands on a visit to town to be able to hazard a guess where his man went after the fracas on Cresset Street. Unless Latter missed his guess, he ought to find the Texan at the General Sheridan Saloon, the eating house or visiting the cathouse out back of town.

While walking along Cresset Street, he saw no sign of a horse that might belong to a Texan standing before any of the business premises; but that did not worry him. Maybe the Texan had left town. Latter hoped not, being a man who hated extra effort in the pursuit of his work. Before he went to the trouble of visiting the livery barn, hiring a horse and riding out of Bainesville, Latter decided to exhaust the town's possibilities first.

Glancing at his pocket-watch, he made for the eating house first. Inside he looked around the almost empty room and knew he had drawn a blank. Heading next for the saloon, as being nearer the less trouble to reach than the cat-house, Latter shoved open the batwing doors and entered. Although he found a fair crowd present, grabbing a holiday and using it to discuss the incident witnessed earlier, the killer saw no sign of the man he sought.

Crossing the room, Latter found a deserted portion of the bar. Leaning on the counter, he summoned service with a commanding jerk of his head. The bartender walked along to where Latter stood, collecting a bottle and glass in passing.

"Where is he?" Latter demanded, after accepting the free drink due to him as a gentleman in the service of prominent citizen Baines Gartree.

"Who?" countered the bartender.

"Don't fuss with me, happen you want to stay working in this town," the killer warned. "You know who."

"You mean that Texan?"

"Naw! Your old drinking-aunt."

"She's back home in Indiana."

"I never could stand lippy help in a bar," Latter growled. "You want for me to talk to your boss?"

"Sure. He's up to Newton."

"I'm asking for the last time," Latter snarled. "Where's that Texan?"

"Him?" answered the bartender, knowing better than push the issue further. "He went off right after the shooting."

"Out of town?" asked Latter, conscious that he now held the attention of every man in the room and that they hung on his words with morbid interest.

"No. With Clint Morley. Looked like he aimed to have his hoss fitted up."

Glancing at the wall-clock, Latter estimated how much time had elapsed since the wounded Gavin Gartree arrived home in his companions' arms.

"They do say that Morley does good work," he said, half to himself.

"Best I've ever seen," admitted the bartender, one of the blacksmith's friends and supporters.

"Takes a longish while to do it, though."

"He's a craftsman," answered the bartender, forgetting the reason behind the statement and springing to his friend's defence. "Any time it's not his best, he don't do it. His sort don't rush their work, but it stays done when they're through."

"Reckon I might still find the Texan there then?"

"You might—if you're looking for him."

"Fill her up again," ordered Latter. "And set them up for the gents here, on Mr. Baines Gartree."

No Western saloon crowd ever refused the offer of a free drink, even if it mostly came with strings attached. Eagerly giving their orders, the crowd watched Latter and wondered what caused the killer's sudden generosity. They found out after the bartender filled their orders and they stood holding drinks.

"You all saw that Texan jump Gavin Gartree and gun him without a chance," Latter announced, his hands making gestures which no range-bred man could fail to understand. Accepting the low mutter as agreement, he went on, "Mr. Gartree wants the man who shot his son bringing in."

"Nobody blames him for that," one of the crowd declared.

"So I'm going to bring him in," Latter continued.

"How about the marshal?" asked the crowd's spokesman, guessing he was expected to do so.

"He's yellow, won't do his duty. Now I say that a man who takes your pay should earn it. If he don't—well, you should take on somebody who will."

Standing outside the batwing doors, Gruber listened to the conversation. He had been on the point of leaving when he learned where he might find the Texan, but stayed to see what game Latter played. From what he had seen of the killer, Gruber knew that the buying of drinks—even at Gartree's expense—was more than a good-will gesture. Clearly the killer meant to improve his position in town and start the voters thinking of their present marshal's failings.

Cold fury filled Gruber as he turned and walked away from the saloon. Up to that moment he had been unsure of whether he ought to take a hand in the forthcoming shooting. Now he knew he must cut in and make sure that Latter did not come through it alive. With that in mind, Gruber entered his office and gave thought to his actions. All too well he knew his limitations in the use of a revolver. He stood no chance at all against a trained gunfighting man like Latter when using a handgun. Not that he intended giving the other anything like a fair chance, but he knew a revolver did not meet his needs. On a rack built against the wall stood the ideal solution to his problem.

Taking down a shotgun from the rack, he broke it and fed in two buckshot-loaded shells. With the law-man's most effective pacifier hung on the crook of his arm, Gruber went out of the rear of the office and, keeping to the rear of the town's outer buildings, made his way towards the blacksmith's forge.

In the saloon, Latter watched the crowd and reckoned that he had done a good piece of work. He finished his drink and smacked his lips appreciatively.

"That come out of the right place," he declared. "Have you any more like it?"

"Sure, a couple of bottles," admitted the bartender reluctantly, knowing his sole remaining stock of a popular brand stood on view behind him.

"They all you've got?"

"Yep."

"Then take 'em down and put them under the

counter. Mr. Gartree'll pay for them and I'll collect them on my way back.''

With that he turned and walked out of the room, conscious of, and a little pleased by, the hum of conversation which rumbled behind him. The bartender watched Latter leave, spat reflectively into a spittoon, replaced the bottle's cork and drove it home with a blow from the heel of his hand. Despite Latter's orders, the bartender made no attempt to remove the other two bottles and place them out of sight. Maybe his job hung in the balance by refusing to obey the orders of Baines Gartree's man; for Latter would be riled if the last two bottles were sold on his return. However, the bartender figured himself free to take such a chance. He had travelled extensively in the West and could claim to be the only person in Bainesville who *knew* the small Texan.

Like a cougar stalking a deer herd, Latter studied his prey as he approached the blacksmith's shop—and saw only the externals.

The Texan looked small, young, undistinguished; the kind of nobody one saw handling the menial chores on some trail drive. Having nothing but contempt for Gavin Gartree's friends, Latter still felt a mite surprised that such a short-grown runt could have chilled their milk; but he put it down to luck. Anyway, he expected no trouble in handling the cowhand. Nor would the other's small size and general air of inconsequence make Gruber look any better in the town's eyes when they thought of the incident.

Of course, with Clint Morley standing by as a witness, Latter knew that he must go through the motions of giving the Texan a fair chance. If it had been any of a number of men around Bainesville standing there, Gartree's name alone would have been enough for Latter to dispense with formalities and drop his victim in the easiest, most convenient manner. The blacksmith was different. Even during the short time Latter served Gartree, he had heard Morley's name mentioned bitterly on more than one occasion. If there was one man in Bainesville with the brains, pull and personality to defeat Gartree in an election campaign, Clint Morley could claim to be he. So far Morley had not interested himself in local politics, but Latter knew that Gartree lived in fear that some day the smith would.

Thinking about Gartree's fears brought up another line. The politician ought to be very grateful for the removal of a dangerous rival. Maybe it would be possible to drop Morley and lay the blame on a wild shot from the Texan's gun. Latter doubted if any coroner's jury would question him too deeply if he pulled it off. Not only would killing Morley earn Gartree's financial gratitude, but also strengthen Latter's hold on the politician. Nobody would believe that he did not act under his employer's orders.

However, before he could reach that stage, he must force a fight with the Texan. Being a hunter, Latter studied his prey and knew the best way to goad it into a fatal charge.

"Hey, beefhead!" he barked, coming to a halt some twenty-five feet from where the Texan stood. "Where'd you get that horse?"

Slowly the Texan turned, moving with almost cat-like alertness so as to be clear of the paint. He expected trouble, for nobody called a son of the Lone Star State by the disparaging name 'beefhead' unless looking for a fight. One glance told the Texan all he needed to know about the speaker.

Not that Latter adopted any fancy, 'menacing' stance; with feet spread, knees slightly bent and right hand hovering with crooked fingers over the Adams' butt. Such, like leaning on the gunbutt, might be the way of an experienced youngster trying to look the part of a tough, fierce, desperate gun fighter. The skilled professional never telegraphed his intentions in such an obvious way. In fact, only a man fully conversant with the gunfighting breed would have read the menace in the way Latter stood. The Texan read it—and prepared to meet the challenge.

"I said where'd you get that paint," Latter repeated.

"What's it to you?" countered the Texan.

"I'm the local law."

"Without a badge?"

"Let's just say that the marshal deputised me and didn't have time to find one."

"Let's say I believe you," drawled the Texan. "In which case, I broke him after he was taken wild in the Ronde River country of Texas."

Mocking disbelief, calculated to infuriate a man likely to be conscious of his lack of heft in a land of big men, came to Latter's face as he looked the Texan over from head to foot.

"*You* broke *that* big horse?"

"I did," agreed the Texan, no sign of anger in his voice, but flat challenge edging his quiet tones.

"Maybe you did—and maybe you didn't," purred Latter. "All I know is that that horse looks mighty like one that Colonel Wilkins bought a piece back. Only I never saw you riding for him."

"I never saw you before, either, *hombre*," drawled the Texan. "But I've seen your kind often enough."

"My kind?" spat Latter.

"Hired guns, *hombre*. Taking pay for killing and not caring how you do it, as long as you do it safe for you. Did Baines Gartree send you after me?"

Latter stiffened a shade, his anger rising at the insult. Then he realised that the Texan was doing to him what he aimed to do to the Texan.

"I came here as a deputy, looking for a horse thi———"

"Now hold that there———" Morley began, but was himself prevented from finishing his speech.

"Leave him be, Clint," the Texan interrupted quietly. "He's been sent after me and I'll take him here and now rather than have him dogging my trail when I ride out. This way he'll have to face me."

Suddenly Morley became aware of a change in the Texan. All the levity and friendliness had gone and a grim, deadly *big* man replaced the easy-going cowhand. In that moment Morley knew that he did not need to intervene. Professional killer Latter might be, but he would not find the Texan easy meat.

Although Latter managed to retain some of his expression of bored competence, fury glowed in his eyes. Such an expression was one of the main weapons in the armoury of a professional killer, conveying an air of certainty that he would be alive at the end of the affair no matter how it turned out for the other. Like Morley, he saw the change in the Texan and for the first time began to realise that mere inches alone did not necessarily make up the man. However, he had gone too far to change his plans for a safer method of handling the Texan.

"I still want to know about that hor———" he started.

"Don't waste my time!" snapped the Texan. "We all know that Gartree sent you after me. Now earn your pay—or get the hell out of my sight."

Never before had a prospective victim acted in such a manner and Gartree felt just a touch uneasy. He realised that he faced the real thing, a man fully conversant with the situation and ready to meet it. Taking the Texan might not be the sinecure Latter fondly imagined.

However, the killer knew a way by which he could gain the vital edge that spelled the difference between life and death.

"I don't know what you're talking about," he said, shrugging his shoulders in an innocent-appearing and disarming manner. "Could be that I've made a mis————"

The shrug changing into a stabbing motion of the right hand in the direction of the Adams' waiting butt. Made with such a preface, the move never failed to give Latter the start he needed.

At Latter's first move gunwards, the Texan's left hand flipped across his body to the white handle of the right side Colt. Even as his lower three fingers curled around the hand-fitting curve of the butt, his thumb closed over the web of the hammer. Like Gartree during his abortive attempt to draw, the Texan began to pull back the hammer immediately—but with one very big difference. So smoothly did the Texan move—and so fast—that the Colt cleared leather before its hammer reached full cock. Nor did the Texan's forefinger enter the triggerguard until the barrel slanted away from him. At no time during the three-quarters of a second it took the Texan to draw and fire his first shot was he in danger from a premature discharge.

Almost everything appeared to be going in Latter's favor. His opening move gave him sufficient start to close his hand on the Adams' butt before the Texan's fingers reached the Colt. With a six inch barrel, the Adams had the advantage of an inch and a half less length to clear its holster and, being double-action, the gun did not require cocking with the thumb before it could fire—although this latter did not prove to be the blessing some observers might expect. Considerable pressure was required to press the Adams' trigger so that it activated the mechanism, causing the hammer to rise to full cock and then snap back on to the waiting percussion cap; far more than required to perform the same operation on the thumb-cocked Army Colt. That factor—along with the Texan's amazing speed—made the Colt just a shade quicker to get off the first shot.

And in such a situation tenths of a second counted.

Flame lashed from the seven and a half inch barrel of the Texan's Army Colt even while the Adams' hammer drew back. Struck in the chest by a conical .44 calibre bullet, Latter jerked back violently. Doing so caused him to swing his gun out of line and when the hammer fell, it sent the bullet out to miss the Texan by a couple of inches.

Although hit by the heavy bullet and staggering under the shock induced by its arrival, Latter kept his feet, retained his hold of the Adams and tried to bring it back into line. Smoothly cocking his Colt, the Texan shot again. He acted without a moment's hesitation, following the way a trained lawman would under the circumstances. Once more lead tore its numbing, agonising way into Latter's body and ripped his heart apart. Uncontrolled fingers opened, the Adams slid free and Latter went down in a limp pile on the ground.

"Watch your left!" Morley bellowed.

Gruber came on the scene at the same time as Latter, but did not make his presence known. Arriving unseen in the alley between two houses some fifty yards from the blacksmith's shop, he made a disturbing discovery. There would be no chance of his moving in any closer, no cover to keep him hidden from Latter and the Texan. Not that Gruber aimed to move in any closer when he could do his work from a safe distance—and, with the shotgun in his hands, he thought he could.

Bringing up the gun, Gruber squinted along the double tubes, aiming the tiny bead foresight on Latter. He did not press the trigger straight away, for he remembered Gartree's orders. Not until after the Texan died at Latter's hands must he cut in. Public sympathy would be on the side of a man who shot down a hired killer; and unlikely to censure the methods used to do so.

Even as Latter started his draw, Gruber squeezed the shotgun's forward trigger. At which point things began to go wrong for the marshal of Bainesville.

Morley never knew just why he happened to glance away from the center of attraction at that particular moment. It may have been that some primeval instinct gave him warning of danger; or a momentary squeamishness in the face of sudden and violent death. Whatever the cause, he turned his head, saw Gruber standing in the background, read the message of the raised shotgun and yelled his warning.

Too late the marshal realised that Latter came off second best in the corpse-and-cartridge affair. Before he could correct his mistake, he heard Morley's shout and spooked like an owl-scared rabbit. Beginning to alter his aim, he saw the Texan whirl to face him, dropping forward to the ground while turning. Then the shotgun bellowed and its burned powder smoke momentarily hid the blacksmith's shop from Gruber's sight.

Nine .32 calibre buckshot balls hissed through the air, spreading out in an invisible, roughly circular pattern which increased in size—and in one way grew less dangerous—with each passing yard. At close range, all nine balls would have found their mark in the Texan's body. As the range increased, so the balls spread out and a lessening number reached their intended destination.

Fifty yards was no range at which to rely on a shotgun in a fight. Nor, if it came to a point, could it be termed an ideal distance to shoot a pistol over when one's life stood as the stake.

In many ways the 1860 Army Colt could claim to be the finest percussion-fired revolver ever manufactured. Built from finest grade materials and by master craftsmen, its mechanism offered simplicity of operation, maintenance and repair. Its streamlined shape gave it smooth handling qualities and its .44 calibre packed the necessary punch to knock a man staggering with a single hit, taking much of the fight out of him. On only one major detail could it be faulted; and it must be admitted that the Army Colt had not been designed for the work its fault entailed. Lacking a top-strap over the cylinder, a formal rear sight could not be fitted and the V-shaped notch carved in the tip of the hammer lip made an indifferent substitute. Such an arrangement did not make for accurate long distance shooting.

However, long training had taught the Texan how to make the most of his gun. Dirt erupted close by where he landed, showing that at least one of the buckshot balls ended its flight harmlessly. Ignoring the sight, the Texan rested his elbows on the ground, supported his left wrist with the right hand and took fast, but careful, aim.

Through the dispersing powdersmoke, even as he drew back the second hammer on his weapon, Gruber saw flame spurt from the Texan's Colt. Something struck under the barrels of the shotgun, jerking it up into the air with considerable force.

Skilled as he might be, the Texan had not shot deliberately to knock the gun from Gruber's hands. At that range, with his life at stake, he could not dare try such fancy gun-work. His bullet had been aimed at Gruber's body, which offered the largest and most easily accessible target. After flying fifty yards, the bullet might have missed completely, but luck guided it to strike the shotgun's barrels.

Luck or not, Gruber knew just how narrow his escape

had been. Somehow he did not relish a duel with a man capable of such devastating skill with a handgun. At any moment he expected the Texan to cut loose again, for he cocked his Colt on its recoil, and doubted if the other would miss a second time.

Throwing aside the gun, Gruber whirled on his heel and fled in panic. Not until the terrified man reached his office did he halt. Entering only long enough to grab his saddle, he left again. At the civic pound, he collected his horse, saddled it in record time and took off to the north as fast as the horse could carry him.

After the marshal's flight, the Texan rose to his feet. Holding his smoking Colt ready for use, he glanced in the direction Gruber took, then swung his eyes towards the still shape on the ground. One look told the Texan that he did not need concern himself with Latter, the killer's days of selling a gun were over. Setting the Colt's hammer down on a safety notch between two of the cylinder's chambers, he slid the weapon back into leather and turned to Morley.

"Thanks for the warning, Clint," he said. "How'll it put you in the town?"

"Gruber won't be back, or I'll be surprised," replied Morley. "And even if he should come, I aim to see that he doesn't keep a badge in Bainesville. He planned to burn you down."

"Could be," admitted the Texan and, having experienced Kansas ideas of justice where his kind were concerned, continued, "Do you reckon the folks hereabouts will want me to stay for a hearing over the killing?"

"Nobody who wants to stay my friend will—and I don't shoe horses or fix things for folks who aren't my friends."

"Don't you go building yourself fuss on my account, Clint."

"You shot in self-defence, and not until after Latter forced the fight on you; which same's no crime in my book," Morley answered. "And nobody'll make me tell it any other way."

"Gartree won't like that," the Texan pointed out.

"I've been thinking for a fair piece now that somebody ought to go against him. Only politics've never been my game. Time comes when a man has to take a stand, happen he wants to be able to look himself in the face."

With that the blacksmith turned and walked to meet the first of the citizens attracted by the sound of the shooting as they came running from the town center. Leaving Morley to tell the new arrivals what happened, the Texan saddled his paint and made ready to ride. From what he saw, the Texan concluded that Morley listened to evidence as well as giving it.

"They wanting to jail me?" asked the Texan, completing the saddling as Morley returned from the crowd.

"Reckon I convinced them that'd lower the tone of the jail," replied the blacksmith. "Fact being that Latter made it clear he was gunning for you. From what he said, he'd set his aim at becoming our town marshal and most folks feel a mite relieved to know they won't have to argue about it with him. None of them'll trouble you any."

"I'll be riding on then," the Texan said. "How much do I owe you?"

After paying for the shoeing of his horse, the Texan shook hands with Morley. "Happen you're ever down in the Rio Hondo country, call in at the ranch and see us, Clint. You'll always find a welcome."

"The same goes for you any time you're up this way. And don't worry about Gartree objecting to your coming."

"I'm not worried about that," answered the Texan,

then his eyes went to where men carried away the killer's body.

"Gartree made a mistake sending him after you," Morley commented.

"It cost him nothing," the Texan replied.

"Reckon you've heard the last of this business?"

"I'd better have," said the Texan grimly. "Will you do something for me, Clint?"

"If I can."

"Go see Gartree. Tell him I'm sorry about what happened to his son, but that it was none of my, or those pilgrims', fault."

"I'll tell him."

"And tell him something else."

"What?"

"You tell Gartree, and make sure he knows I mean every word I say, that happen he spreads lies about what came off today—or if he ever sends another hired gun after me—I'll come back here and make him wish he'd never been born."

"I'll do just that," promised the blacksmith and, although he could guess at the answer, went on. "Who should I tell him sent the message, happen he wants to know."

A faint smile played on the small Texan's lips as he swung afork the paint stallion. Not until mounted and ready to move off did he reply. His words verified Morley's suspicions and cleared up a number of points. He said:

"Tell him Dusty Fog."

CHAPTER SIX

Travellers on the South-Bound Trail

Dusty Fog. The name meant much to people on the Western shores of the Mississippi and most of all to citizens of the Lone Star State. While dwellers in Austin County might claim Bad Bill Longley as the fastest hand with a gun ever to breathe Texas air, or Panhandle citizens lay the same claim on Clay Allison, a point disputed hotly by John Wesley Hardin's supporters in the Mount Calm district, and the devotees of many another local hero, those same swift-handed heroes admitted, if only to themselves, that Dusty Fog stood at the head of their particular claim to fame.

Yet there was more, much more, than just a lightning fast draw and deadly accurate aim to account for the general acceptance of Dusty Fog as Texas' favorite son.

While speaking to Morley, the casual reference to 'my company' had been the truth. At seventeen Dusty Fog assumed Command of Company "C", Texas Light Cavalry, and led it to such purpose that—while fighting on the less-publicised Arkansas battle-front—he built a name as a military raider equal to those other Dixie masters, Turner Ashby and John Singleton Mosby.*

* Told in *The Fastest Gun in Texas, The Devil Gun, The Colt and the Sabre.*

At the end of the War, Dusty returned to Texas; although no less a man than General Ulysses S. Grant offered him a place in the Union Army with his C.S.A. rank and seniority. Instead of falling into a slough of self-pity over the South's defeat, Dusty forgot the past and became fully involved in rebuilding the mighty OD Connected ranch. At nineteen, he found himself riding into war-torn Mexico on a mission and with the future peace of the United States in his young hands. †

Bringing the mission to a successful conclusion did not lead to a life of leisure and peace. Since that time, Dusty Fog's name had gone forth as a tophand with cattle, segundo of the biggest, most efficient and profitable ranch in Texas, trail boss second to none, the town-taming lawman of the finest kind. Men told tales of his uncanny bare-handed techniques of fighting, which rendered bigger and stronger opponents helpless before him; for this added yet another claim to Dusty Fog's fame.

Such then was the identity and history of the small, insignificant man who had just concluded a hectic visit to Bainesville, Kansas, and provided the town with conversational material for months to come.

Holding his big paint to a steady four-mile-an-hour walk, Dusty headed in a southerly direction. Business had taken him to Eastern Kansas at the conclusion of a successful trail drive and his way home took him through the rolling land which rarely saw Texas cowhands, it being off the line taken by the north-bound herds. Fear of Gartree's vengeance did not cause Dusty to ride. Down in the Indian Nations, at Duke Bent's hospitable establishment, two loyal friends waited for him to join them. Loyal they might be, but he

† Told in *The Ysabel Kid*.

knew that the Ysabel Kid and Mark Counter would wax
sarcastic and suggest slanderous reason for his tardiness
should he arrive later than his proposed date.

There was another reason for Dusty allowing his
paint to stride out and make the most of his capacity for
swift, continuous travel. Somewhere ahead of him, the
wagon carrying the people his intervention saved from
young Gartree rolled south. While Dusty did not wish to
be thanked for what he had done in Bainesville, he felt it
might be pleasant to see the little blonde girl again.

The trail Dusty followed wound along the line of
what, until only a few years previously, had been a buffalo migration route. One could trust the great, shaggy
beasts to know the easiest line of march, although the
direction they took did not often follow a straight line.
As he rode, Dusty thought of the scene as the great
herds moved across the range. It must have been much
like a trail herd, except that no men rode along to keep
the animals pointed in the right direction. Nor had any
trail herd ever been of such numbers as the mass of buffalo which carved the trail. Yet now they were gone for
ever, shot for meat, for their tongues, hides and even
for sport. Not even the bones remained, having been
gathered up and sold. Born in an age which ignored
animal preservation, Dusty still felt compassion and a
little sorrow as he thought of the slaughter of the buffalo. Yet as a cattleman, he knew that the great buffalo
herds could not be allowed to roam at will. Their vast
numbers offered too much competition with the cattle
and an enormous herd could spread over the land,
smashing down all before it by weight of numbers.
Slaughter seemed to be the only answer as Dusty knew.
The knowledge did not make him feel any better.

At the top of each ridge, Dusty scanned the trail
ahead in the hope of seeing the wagon. While he was

disappointed in that, he found that other people used the south-bound trail.

Four riders held their horses to a steady walk about half a mile ahead of him. Halting his paint, Dusty studied the quartet and decided that three of them looked decidedly familiar. Recognising the Cooper brothers and Lanny, Dusty disliked the implication their presence brought to mind. Nor did he require the second-sight of a Comanche witch-woman to guess at the identity of the fourth rider. Seeing the tip of the holster under Gartree's coat, Dusty needed little mental effort to decide what took the politician out of town and sent him along the trail to the south.

"I might be doing them an injustice, old horse," he told the paint, after forming his conclusions, "but I sure as hell doubt it."

With that in mind, he turned the paint's head and left the trail at a forty-five degrees angle. The big stallion had the legs of any of the quartet's mounts. Even the horse Gartree rode, fine beast though it might be, could not out-pace Dusty's paint; especially when carrying the politician who did not ride light in his saddle. So, while he did not doubt that he could overtake the men, Dusty did not intend to do it by passing them on the trail and presenting them with a chance to shoot him in the back.

There might be some simple, innocent reason for Gartree taking a trip, but Dusty doubted it. Even should it be so, he knew that a man like Gartree would not pass up the opportunity to extract vengeance for the crippling of his son. Not wanting to tangle in another gun-fight, for he never took killing lightly, Dusty intended to swing around any possible trouble. He also wished to catch up with the wagon, for he believed that the four men intended to do just that with the intention of avenging young Gartree.

Once off the trail, Dusty gave the paint its signal to change from a walk to trot. Underfoot the grass grew short and springy, offering a more gentle surface than the hard-packed earth of the trail. The course he took swung him away from Gartree's party and into country which he figured would serve to keep him hidden from their sight.

During the War, on missions inside Federal-held territory, Dusty had learned the art of unseen movement through hostile country. Peace had never been so complete for him that he lost the knack gained during the wild days when he led Company 'C' in raids which became classic studies of light cavalry tactics. Of course, the situation Dusty found himself involved in on the trail out of Bainesville could not be compared with the War. The men he sought to avoid did not expect trouble, had no suspicion of his presence and consequently were not on the alert.

The paint stallion strode out, covering the ground at a steady six-miles-an-hour trot; a better pace than the four men on the trail made. Although keeping to a line roughly parallel to the trail, Dusty sometimes had to make a detour to avoid a natural hazard over which he could not ride in safety. A master horseman, Dusty knew exactly what risks he could take, when he could ride without chancing injury to his mount, or when he must walk.

During the remainder of the afternoon, Dusty rode steadily south. On the occasions when he took up a hidden position and studied the trail, he hoped for a sight of the wagon. However, with over a two hour start, the travellers had built up a good lead and he saw nothing of them. Nor, if it came to a point, did he see any sign of the quartet of riders after the first hour or so. Travelling faster than Gartree's bunch and keeping

moving, Dusty soon found himself beyond any chance
of them seeing him. However, he did not return to the
trail, but kept off it and out of the view of any chance-
passing travellers. He had no desire to meet people
journeying to Bainesville, for such could be almost
guaranteed to want to stop and talk. Nor would they
restrict their conversation to him. Wishing to keep his
presence unsuspected, Dusty did not want some chance-
met stranger carrying word back to Gartree that a small
Texan on a big paint stallion rode ahead.

Shortly before night came, Dusty saw that he would
be compelled to return to the trail. Curving down, the
gash torn originally by the buffalo entered an area of
thickly wooded country. He knew that the travellers
could not be far ahead and figured to join them
wherever they decided to camp for the night. After a
careful study of his back-trail, even though he doubted
that Gartree's crowd would be close enough to see him,
Dusty rode in cover as much as possible and slipped
cautiously back on to the trail just inside the woods.
Fresh horse-droppings on the track ahead of him told
him that he was not far behind the travellers.

For a short time Dusty walked his paint along the trail
which now wound and curved through flowering dogwood, white oak, paper birch and tuliptrees. Scattered
among the larger growth, sassafras shrub and other
bushes grew thick enough to stop Dusty seeing what lay
around the next bend.

The scent of wood-smoke wafted back on the breeze,
coming to Dusty's nostrils even as his ears picked up the
faint rattle of metal against metal. As yet he could see
nothing, for the trail curved off around a bend.
Dismounting, Dusty led his paint into the trees and clear
of the trail. Earlier, during his final approach to the
woods, he had found a stream and allowed the horse to

drink its fill, so knew a short wait without attention would cause it little or no suffering.

After loosening the saddle's girth enough to allow the blood to gradually circulate in the paint's back, Dusty fastened the reins to a tree. Patient training had taught the horse not to roll on the ground while saddled and Dusty did not need to worry on that score. With his horse's immediate needs handled, Dusty drew the Winchester from its saddle-boot. Compact, light, handy, with a magazine capacity of thirteen rounds, the twenty-inch barrelled carbine would be more suitable than his matched Army Colts should his suspicions of Gartree's motives prove correct.

While Dusty could not claim to be as expert as his good friend the Ysabel Kid in the art of silent movement through wooded country in darkness, he managed to move in the direction from which the wood-smoke originated without making too much noise. Placing his feet down carefully, feeling for anything that might snap under it, or turn and cause him to slip, while avoiding brushing against branches that could rustle in the still of the night, Dusty literally followed his nose until he saw the red glow of a fire among the trees ahead. Even as he caught his first glimpse of the fire, Dusty noticed a series of short, brilliant white flashes such as lightning might make in its path across the skies. Only the flickers came more regularly than those caused by storm-brought lightning and without the accompaniment of rain or rolling thunder. Also the flashes seemed to originate from down at ground level and close to where the fire glowed.

While moving on through the trees, Dusty wondered what might be causing the intermittent white glowing, for he could not remember having seen its like before.

The nearest to it in Dusty's experience had come from the flare of magnesium powder when used by photographers to illuminate their subject when taking a picture. Yet even magnesium powder did not produce such regular, short or brilliant flashes.

Still trying to reach a conclusion about the flashing, Dusty reached the edge of the trees and halted. Ahead of him lay a large clearing. Close to the banks of the stream which, higher up its course, served to water Dusty's paint, the wagon stood. To one side of the wagon, kneeling by a fire, the girl dropped something into a steaming pan set on the flames. The elder man led the horses towards the stream, but Dusty could see no sign of the younger.

It might have been an ordinary camp scene that Dusty looked upon, except for the inexplicable flashes of light which appeared to come from inside the wagon. Watching the flashes, which showed through the raised flap of the wagon's canopy, Dusty felt even more puzzled. No kerosene-fed lamp ever attained such brightness and the flashes had an almost mechanical regularity which reminded him of heliograph messages flashing across country during the War.

Standing hidden among the trees, Dusty was just about to make his presence known when the flashing stopped. He heard the sound of a wooden lid being closed and saw the girl turn from the fire. Leaving her cooking, she walked over to where the younger of the men jumped down from the rear of the wagon. On landing, the man allowed the covers to drop back into place, then turned to the girl. It almost seemed as if they held a conversation, yet neither said a word that Dusty could hear. The girl swung her head in the direction of the elder man and he left the horses to join his companions.

Even then, although the trio gave the impression of discussing something, Dusty still could neither hear words nor see their lips move.

For a moment Dusty wondered if he ought to call out a greeting, then go and give the travellers a warning of their danger. Not wishing to raise a false alarm, he decided to check on his suspicions before making an appearance at the camp. Turning, he faded back into the woods and left the trio still standing in that silent attitude of conversation.

Deciding that the trail would be dark enough for him to chance using it rather than moving through the trees, Dusty walked slowly back from the clearing. One man on foot ought to avoid detection from a quartet riding horses. He figured he should be able to locate Gartree's party early enough for him to hide and make his arrangements.

All around the normal night noises came to Dusty's ears. A disturbed bird fluttered from a bush close at hand, twittering in alarm until it found another place to roost. Overhead a whip-poor-will sent out its plaintive call as it hunted the flying insects on which it fed. Down to the south, in the far distance, a Great Plain buffalo wolf raised a howl to gather others of its kind. Coyotes yipped eerily from three sides of the wooded area. Only from the north came no calls of the little prairie scavengers—the significance of which Dusty understood.

Hunted at every turn by human beings, the wily coyote learned early to avoid its two-legged enemy and rarely gave a sign of its presence when men were about. So Dusty took note of the lack of noise in the direction of the Bainesville trail and did not need to guess at the cause.

The sound of horses' hooves came to Dusty's ears and then voices, although at first too distant for him to understand the words. When the speakers came closer, what he heard confirmed his theories and started him advancing cautiously towards the approaching riders. Leather creaked after the hooves halted and Dusty moved closer. A cold, grim smile came to his lips—and any member of the OD Connected ranch crew would have known the expression, then felt sorry for the men who caused it—as he changed his plans a little, preparing to handle the matter in what he regarded as the most fitting manner.

CHAPTER SEVEN

Two Heroes Develop Feet of Clay

Bringing his horse to a halt, Baines Gartree eased his aching body and peered through the darkness at the gloomy gap where the trail ran into the woods. Unused to the rigours of long travel on the back of a horse, the ride from Bainesville served to put a considerable damper on his desire for revenge.

"We've seen no sign of them yet," he complained. "Maybe they didn't come down this way after all."

"They said they were going south, and this's south," replied Turkey Cooper, slouching in his saddle and scowling at the politician.

"They could have turned off the trail back there and gone across country."

"Pilgrims like that bunch don't go across country when they can stick to a clear, well-marked trail. And there's been no wagon tracks going off the trail—I've been watching for 'em."

"Trust old Turkey for that," grinned Lanny, full of hero-worship as always.

"He knows what he's doing, for sure," agreed Coop.

"But we don't know———" began Gartree.

"We know they left town by the south trail and they haven't pulled off it," said Turkey. "Can't remember passing their wagon on the way, neither, can you, Brother Coop?''

"If we did, I figure I might've noticed," answered Coop.

"Well, I think we ought to have caught up with them by now," Gartree put in, seething with rage at the young men's disrespect. "Or at least seen some sign of them on the trail ahead of us."

"And we might have, if you hadn't kept slowing us down," Turkey replied.

"There's a clearing maybe half—three-quarters of a mile ahead in the woods," Lanny commented. "That's where they'll have made their camp for the night, most likely. Them not knowing this range and all."

"I can't see any sign of their fire," Gartree objected.

"You're not likely to, from here and through all them trees!" snorted Turkey in a disgusted voice. "The clearing's there all right, and I'll bet that's where we find those pilgrims."

"All right then," Gartree said, fighting to keep the anger from showing in his voice. "We'll push on to the clearing. But if they're not in it, we'll———"

"Decide what we aim to do next," interrupted Turkey, starting his horse moving without waiting for further comment.

The other two young men followed on Turkey's heels, crowding Gartree forward between them. Although the politician hated being treated in such a manner, he knew better than voice his objections aloud. Being handled with such disrespect did nothing to lessen his resolve to carry out the plans made for dealing with the trio after they had served their purpose. A word in Gruber's ear on their return to Bainesville, telling of the attack on the travellers—without of course mentioning Gartree's part in it—would be sufficient. No man in the West would condone insult or assault committed on a girl and justice was likely to be swift, if not all-embracing. Gartree doubted if any of the trio would be given a chance to mention his part in the affair, so swift would be their end. Of course, he must handle the affair properly and ensure that the Coopers and Lanny died before they could tell their story. Thinking of the town marshal's lack of aptitude, Gartree almost wished that he had kept Latter alive to handle the business.

Further thoughts on the matter ended as Turkey, riding in the lead of the party for the first time, halted his horse.

"I can smell smoke ahead," the young man announced. "There's somebody nighting in the clearing."

"What do we do, Turkey?" asked Lanny eagerly.

"Let's charge in like a drunk Sioux coming to a pow-wow," suggested Coop.

"No we don't!" snapped Turkey. "We're leaving the horses here and moving up on tippy-toe."

"Why bother sneaking up?" Lanny inquired. "We won't have any trouble handling pilgrims like them."

"Maybe not," admitted Turkey. "But a ten gauge kills just as good in a Bible-toting pilgrim's hands."

"Never saw no sign of guns on 'em back in town," Coop remarked, having a cowhand's dislike for walking, even though he had never worked on a ranch.

"That young jasper acted like he aimed to go for the wagon and get one when Gav jumped the gal," Turkey pointed out. "And I've yet to see one of them pilgrim outfits who didn't tote a gun along, even if only to use for shooting table-meat."

"We don't even know that it is them ahead," Gartree said, feeling he ought to make some addition to the conversation.

"Which same the senator's got him a real good

point," conceded Turkey, sounding considerably surprised that Gartree could think out such a profound remark. "It wouldn't do for us to go charging in head-down and horns hooking, then find we'd jumped the wrong outfit."

Recalling the last time they jumped into something without making an adequate study of the opposition, Coop and Lanny felt inclined to agree with Turkey.

"Best leave the hosses here then," Coop stated.

"Now you're beginning to use your head for something besides a hat-rack," Turkey sniffed and dismounted. "Here's a right good place to leave them."

The quartet had come to a halt alongside a large flowering dogwood tree which glowed a faint, ghostly white as what little light remained filtered down to reflect from its blossom-hung branches. Such a tree, the only one of its kind directly flanking the trail, would serve as a marker leading them straight back to their horses.

Dismounting, the men fastened their horses to handy protuberances. Gartree opened his mouth to make a protest, but, beyond snarling for quiet, Turkey ignored him. It became clear who now commanded the vengeance-seeking party. On leaving town, and for the first part of the ride, the trio at least made a pretence at letting Gartree command them. After all, the brand of politics he gave out ideally suited their shiftless, work-shy natures, and they felt that he must be a good man for that reason. The farther they travelled in his company, the less their respect for him became. With the waning of Gartree's command over the quartet, so Turkey's rose. More and more Coop and Lanny came to listen to Turkey rather than Gartree. At last they had made the step and gone over completely behind the young man they regarded as a hero.

If he had been given to thinking, Coop might have
wondered at his brother's motives for accepting Gartree's request to take revenge. Generosity, largeness of
heart and loyalty to a friend did not figure so large in
Turkey's make-up that he would take a long ride merely
to extract revenge on somebody who indirectly caused a
companion's injury. However, it never occurred to
Coop that he might question his elder brother's motives.
If he had, Coop would have received a surprise—always
assuming that Turkey told him the truth.

Realising that they would no longer be able to live
high off the hog at Gavin Gartree's expense, Turkey
sought for a means of raising a decent grub-stake that
might last them until they found another source of
work-free income. He discarded the idea of robbing any
of the Bainesville businesses as too dangerous. However, the three pilgrims offered no such challenge.
Rumour credited all the small religious groups which
drifted about the range country with possessing large
sums of money secreted in their wagons. With that
thought in mind, Turkey readily gave his agreement to
ride and avenge young Gartree. Knowing what he
planned, Turkey wanted no witnesses and never thought
to have Gartree senior on his hands. After some
thought, he decided that the politician's presence did
him nothing but good. Gartree could not talk to the law
without exposing his own part in the affairs and would
have to use his authority to prevent any close investiga-
tion by the law coming close to them. In the future, too,
Gartree ought to be a regular source of wealth rather
than have his part in the affair made public.

The men moved in silence along the trail, each busy
with his thoughts and none showing any great alertness.
While Gartree planned the removal of the three young
men on their return to Bainesville, Coop and Lanny

savoured the pleasure of jumping the pilgrims' camp, and Turkey thought of the easy life lying ahead as a result of judicious blackmail to bring in wealth. Then all thoughts of the future came to a sudden halt.

"Listen!" hissed Turkey, stopping and swinging around to look in the direction from which they came.

Obeying the command, all the others heard the sound of departing hooves.

"One of the horses has got loose!" announced Gartree dramatically—and completely unnecessarily.

"And another!" yelped Lanny as the drumming of horse's hooves repeated itself on the trail behind them.

"I fastened mine up ri————" began Coop.

"Get back to them—quick!" Turkey snarled and led the rush, for already there came the noise of another horse departing.

The thought of a ten miles walk back to Bainesville lent urgency to the quartet's movements and prevented them thinking of certain aspects of the affair. Once free, a hungry range horse, riderless and started moving, would head back to where it knew food could be found. Home to the four animals was the livery barn in Bainesville, or the stables behind Gartree's house. It was unlikely that any of the freed horses would stop before reaching the town. Certainly they would not stop for some distance and then not for long.

Thinking about the walk took the other problem from their minds. Not one of the quartet came to think how four horses managed to free themselves and light out for home.

Running along the dark path, each man tried to keep up his hopes that his ears tricked him, or at worst only the other three's horses had escaped. At last, as they approached the flowering dogwood tree, all accepted the bitter truth. The four horses ought to be standing close by, secured and patiently awaiting their riders' return. No waiting mounts greeted the four searching pairs of eyes.

"What the hell happ———" Gartree began.

With the faint sibilant hiss of sound an owl's wings made as it flitted through the darkness, something passed over the politician's head and dropped in a circle about him. Before his startled mind could form any conclusions and react to a possible danger, he felt his legs dragged together by the constriction of some thin, mysterious substance which encircled his ankles. Just as he realised that the thing gripping his legs was a rope, which must have a human agency handling it, Gartree felt a violent tug, lost his balance and started to fall. In desperation, he threw his arms around Coop and brought the young man down with him. Never one to suffer alone, Coop contrived to lay hands on Lanny and add him to the already growing heap of humanity upon the trail.

Hearing the commotion behind him, Turkey whirled around and reached for his gun. He did not know what might be happening, but guessed that it boded evil for his party.

Instead of jumping Gartree's party as they approached him, Dusty Fog had conceived a far worse punishment; probably the worst, short of death, to spring to the mind of a man raised on the great Texas range country. Even without the verbal confirmation, the quartet's action proved their intentions. Men on a peaceable and well-disposed mission did not leave their horses and move in on foot when approaching a camp at night. So Dusty figured to teach them a lesson they would never forget.

Standing unseen among the bushes, Dusty watched the four men go by and then moved silently along the

trail in the direction from which they came. Taking a
knife from his pocket, Dusty approached the horses. A
low, gentle and soothing whisper checked any restive-
ness the horses might have shown and he moved alongside the first animal ready to put through his plan.
Thrusting the carbine into his gunbelt to leave his hands
free, Dusty severed the horse's reins close to the bit. A
range horse was trained to stand when its reins hung free
before it and he wished to ensure that the freed mounts
had nothing to halt them.

After freeing the first horse and starting it moving,
Dusty turned his attention to the second. His knife
sliced through the leather and he sent the horse on its
way after its companion. Just as Dusty reached the third
animal, he heard voices raised along the trail and knew
that Gartree's party had heard the departure of the first
two.

Stepping along the flank of the last horse, Dusty felt a
familiar object brush against his shoulder. A thought of
how he might cause further devilment struck him and he
pulled free the rope from its place on the saddle's horn.
Swiftly he cut the last horse free and found little difficulty in starting it moving after the others. By that
time he knew he must move fast, for the four men returned hurriedly although not yet in view. Sliding free
the carbine, Dusty crossed the trail and halted alongside
the sturdy trunk of a big white oak tree which offered
cover and protection. No sooner had the small Texan
taken his place than Turkey led the others into sight of
the flowering dogwood.

Dusty rested his carbine against the tree trunk and
close to his hand. Shaking out the coils of the rope, he
opened out a loop and watched the approaching quartet
with calculating eyes. Being a good leader, Turkey came
slightly in advance of the others—or more likely he

intended to lay claim should only one horse remain under the dogwood tree. Dusty checked his impulse to throw at Turkey, deciding that a better target for his attentions would be presented by the closely-bunched trio following the leader.

Allowing Turkey to pass unmolested Dusty watched until the other three came level and gave the rope a quick, deft twirl which caused its loop to rise up before him. Like an extension of his arm, the thirty foot length of seven-sixteenths of an inch hard-plaited Manila rope sailed out and away, its loop spreading and turning parallel to the ground as if possessing a mind of its own. Through necessity—handling a strange rope which had not been cared for or used as much as his own—Dusty threw a much larger loop than he usually employed. Working in darkness prevented him from tossing a small, neat hooley-ann loop and anyway that particular throw would not have served his needs under the circumstances; being a head catch primarily intended for snaking selected horses out of a crowded corral without spooking the remainder of the animals. Instead he threw what might have been termed a "belly-rope," although it would be unfair to give so disparaging a name to a throw which brought about such a splendid result; the belly rope being so called when thrown with a loop too large so that it slipped over the sought-after animal's head and shoulders to tighten about its midsection, highly amusing to the onlookers but not to the thrower.

Aiming at Gartree, whose white shirt showed up well even in the darkness and made him by far the most prominent target, Dusty knew he threw true. When the rope fell, the small Texan gripped hold with both hands and hauled back on it. He used a fair amount of strength, feeling the rope slip through the honda until it clamped around Gartree's legs. Then Dusty really threw

all his powerful effort into a heave which brought about
the results already noted.

Even as the three men went down in a tangled, curs-
ing, shouting heap, Dusty dropped the rope and stepped
behind the white oak's trunk. Catching up the carbine in
passing, he prepared to handle it from his left side and
took up a position accordingly behind the tree trunk. He
raised the carbine, keeping most of his body in cover,
and took aim towards the trail.

Consternation reigned before Dusty as the three men
fell in a tangle. Some fairly inspired invective rose, in-
terspersed by demands for information from the still
standing Turkey. Dusty allowed the first flow to die
down before making his presence more definitely
known.

"Fun's over for the day!" he announced. "Now it's
time to get up and start walking home."

Recognition of the soft, easy drawling voice came to
Turkey first. Snarling with fury, the young man realised
his fears had had good founding. When he heard the
shooting back at Bainesville, certain significant points
sprang to his mind. The first shot came from an Army
Colt such as the small Texan carried, followed by one
with the lighter note of the Adams Latter wore. Which
meant the Texan got off the first shot and, if Turkey
remembered correctly, also the third. Then another
Army Colt's detonation followed on the heels of the
shotgun's blast, but no more sounds to show that Latter
still remained an active participant in the fight. Turkey
had been afraid that the Texan might be still alive, but
comforted himself with the thought that a shotgun,
properly used, only rarely missed doing its work.

Clearly Marshal Gruber botched up his duty, as he
had done on so many previous occasions, for the Texan
still lived. Worse, that soft speaking, deadly efficient

young man stood close by, having already disrupted Turkey's party and set them afoot.

Jerking out his Colt, Turkey threw a shot in the direction of the voice and sent it with some accuracy, for the lead struck the tree behind which Dusty stood. Not that the Texan had any need to feel concerned; the white oak's trunk had bulk enough to stop the bullet of a Sharps Old Reliable or Remington Creedmoor buffalo rifle and the Army Colt lacked their power. In fact the shot fired at him served a very useful purpose.

Using the Colt's muzzle-blast as his guide, Dusty triggered off three shots in a second and a half. The lead ripped by Turkey's head, making that spine-chilling "splat!" sound as they shattered through the air. While posing as a big, hard man, and seeking the honoured name of gun-fighting killer, Turkey had never been under fire before, nor heard the unnerving sound of close-passing lead. Never a pleasant sound, the passing bullets had a shocking impact when coupled with the spurts of flame which erupted from the darkness. Already half-blinded by the glare given out by burning powder from his own gun, Turkey could only stand and stare. Suddenly, shockingly, Turkey realised his precarious position. Standing out in the open, he was completely at the mercy of the unseen man with the deadly carbine. While the first three shots missed, they came close enough to him for him to realise that they were not intended to hit. Even if luck guided them by him, Turkey figured that his good fortune could not last against ten more bullets that the carbine most likely held. At that moment Turkey's nerve snapped. Throwing aside his gun, he turned and fled as fast as he could go along the trail down which he rode so cheerily on his quest for loot and revenge.

On the ground, the three men managed to untangle themselves and roll apart. While shaken by their fall and the sudden blasting of shots, not one of the trio failed to grasp the full seriousness of their position.

"What the———" Gartree began, then, realising he was in no position to make demands, moderated his tone. "Who are you?"

"Your hired men missed out in Bainesville, *hombre*," replied a Texan drawl, chilling under its easy flow.

Raw fear bit into Gartree as he understood the implication of the words. He knew that Latter and Gruber between them failed to kill the young Texan and now he stood there in the darkness, most likely lining his carbine and starting to squeeze its trigger.

"Don't shoot!" he screeched. "I never sent them after you."

"Neither the hired gun nor the marshal?"

"If either of them said I did, they lied!"

"I killed your hired man, he went without talking, Mr. Gartree, and likely your tame marshal's not stopped running yet."

"D—Don't shoot me!" Gartree moaned.

Fury welled up inside Coop as he saw the second of his heroes show feet of clay. Always he regarded Turkey as the bravest of the brave and only lacking a chance to prove himself—and given his opportunity, Turkey showed a yellow streak, threw aside his gun and fled. There had been a time also when Coop regarded Gartree as a hero, a gallant defender of the under-dog who dared stand up to lawmen and make them look small. Yet that same defiant hero now cringed and begged not to be hurt, after sending hired killers to do his dirty work.

Rage at his brother and Gartree drove Coop to rash

wildness. He wanted to show the Texan that at least one man had the courage to stand against him.

"Damn it to hell!" Coop screeched, thrusting himself to his feet. "Come on out where we can see you and make your fight."

CHAPTER EIGHT

Captain Fog Speeds Departing Guests

The last thing Dusty wanted to do was kill either Coop or Lanny. During his time as a lawman,* Dusty had seen many young men like the pair on the trail. They were products of their times, living in a hard land, fed on stories of the escapades of the gun-fighting breed. Some instinct told Dusty that the two young men were more likely to follow than be leaders; and he could understand Coop's feeling, so knew why the other made that reckless challenge.

"You can have it that way if you want," the small Texan said calmly. "Just say the word and let loose your wolf."

"No!" screamed Gartree, just as Dusty figured he would. "Don't do it!"

Raw, unadulterated panic filled the politician's voice and bit like a knife into Lanny. Less affected by the failure of Turkey than Coop had been, Lanny saw only the gravity of their situation and realised the futility of challenging a man armed with a Winchester—which he could obviously use with skill and precision—when carrying only a revolver. At that moment Lanny remem-

* Told in *Quiet Town* and *The Trouble Busters*.

bered the number of times both he and Coop missed
their mark when shooting their guns. He doubted if the
Texan lacked skill; in fact, seeing that the other came
through a fight against a professional killer and a
shotgun-armed marshal, had no doubts in the matter at
all. True the Texan's weapon sounded like a carbine,
but that gave Lanny little or no comfort. While the carbine version of the "Old Yellowboy" carried only thirteen bullets in its magazine, plus one in the chamber, as
opposed to the rifle's sixteen, a skilled man could fire it
at a rate of two shots a second. The Texan was skilled,
and his carbine held enough bullets, even after disposing
of Turkey, to make things mighty exciting should he
come out in answer to Coop's challenge.

"Don't be crazy, Coop!" the youngster hissed. "We
wouldn't have a chance."

"Best listen to him," Dusty warned, staying in cover.
"He's speaking the best sense you're ever likely to
hear."

Slowly the fighting madness ebbed out of Coop and
sense returned. Not until then did he realise how foolish
his challenge had been and see what Lanny already
knew. Yet he felt reluctant to back down without
making some token resistance.

"How about it?" asked Dusty, timing his words just
right so that they came before Coop reached a second
stage of defiance. "Do we make a fight?"

"No!" howled Gartree and Lanny echoed the words.

"That's only two of you," Dusty commented.

"I don't want a fight," admitted Coop bitterly.

"Then throw your gunbelts this way."

"Like hell!" Coop snarled.

"It's your choice. But I aim to have the gunbelts and
if you give me fuss, I'll take your pants—and boots too."

Probably the last threat, more than any other, decided the issue. Hearing the cold, deadly purpose underlying the easy drawl and knowing the Texan possessed the means to enforce his demands—not one of the trio doubted that Dusty intended to carry out his words. Faced with the consequences of refusal, either shooting it out with the Texan or walking barefoot to town, only one course remained open.

"This's robbery————" Gartree began in a wavering voice, starting to unbuckle his belt.

"And I'm getting mighty shy on patience," Dusty replied. "Which is it to be?"

"Don't shoot!" Gartree repeated in a panic-filled screech. "I'm doing what you want!"

With that, he unhitched his belt and threw it into the blackness, relief oozing through him as he heard it thud against the oak's trunk. Lanny peeled off his belt and followed Gartree's example, guessing that the Texan would not shoot down an unarmed man. That left Coop; and Dusty knew of the trio the young man was most likely to try something.

Still smarting under the humiliation of failure, Coop reached for and unbuckled his gunbelt. Before obeying Dusty's order, he slipped the Colt from its holder and kept it in his hand as he flung the belt into the blackness.

"Now toss the gun after it," Dusty said, for the belt's arrival did not have the correct, solid sound.

"What g————?" began Coop.

A bullet tore into the ground within a couple of inches of Coop's right foot and caused him to make a rapid leap to the rear.

"Don't play games with me," Dusty ordered, working the carbine's lever.

"What if Injuns jump us?" Coop yelped, not wanting to give in and wishing he could summon up the courage to use his gun.

"It's been many a long year since the last hostiles came this far east," Dusty pointed out.

"There's bears and cougar———"

"Toss it over and leave them tend to their own affairs."

Despite the light note, Coop detected a subtle change in Dusty's voice and knew that he had pushed the Texan as far as was safe. Going beyond that point invited disaster and if he took the business further, must take it to the bitter end. Knowing what the end would most likely be, Coop growled out a low, bitter curse and hurled his gun forward. He heard metal strike wood and clatter to the ground. The sound carried all the bitter finality of defeat.

A low sigh of relief left Gartree at the sound. The politician felt much safer once all his party's weapons had been discarded. Like Lanny, Gartree knew the Texan was not likely to open fire on unarmed men.

"I don't know what your reason is for this outrage," Gartree stated, putting on a tone of injured innocence which had served him well at other times when his veracity or motives had been called into question. "What do you want with us?"

"What're *you* wanting, mister?" countered Dusty.

"Can't a man take a ride along a trail without being suspect?"

"Why sure. As long as he isn't suspect."

"I had to ride south on business."

"Important business?" asked Dusty.

"Real important," agreed Gartree. "To do with the affairs of the State Legislature."

"Now that is important," said Dusty, sounding suitably impressed.

"It is."

"I admire a man who'd leave his sick son to ride on his voters' business. Only I don't believe a word of it. What'd you aim to do when you caught up with those pilgrims?"

"Pilgrims?"

"The three camped in the clearing," Dusty explained.

"Camped in the clearing?" repeated Gartree, trying to retain his innocence. "Which clear————"

"You know what I mean. The camp you aimed to jump because you blame the folks in it for your son getting hurt."

"We didn't aim to do anything to them," Lanny put in. "We didn't even know it was them————"

"I'm asking Mr. Gartree," Dusty interrupted.

"We saw the fire and decided to go in for a meal and spend the night by the stream," Gartree declared.

"Only that?" asked Dusty.

"Nothing more."

"Mister," Dusty drawled, irony plain in his voice. "Happen you lie like that all the time, you'll make Congress for sure."

"I don't know————" Gartree began.

"I do," Dusty told him. "I know why you came down here, what you figured on doing to those folks—and can guess what you meant to do to those three fellers who came with you."

"What's that supposed to mean?" asked Coop sullenly.

"Do you figure that he aimed to let you get away with letting his son be crippled—especially after what you planned to do tonight?"

"You're way ahead of me, mister," Coop said, showing enough interest for Dusty to carry on.

"Look at how he tried to handle everybody else involved. He sent his killer after me, and the marshal. Then he brought you along to fix those pilgrims. Do you think he aimed to forget that you three didn't stop me jumping his boy?''

A slight pause followed Dusty's words, pregnant with thought for the two young men and filled with anxiety for Gartree.

"You reckon that he————" began Lanny, then trailed off as he could not think of how Gartree might take revenge on him after accompanying the trio on their revenge mission.

"Look at it this way," Dusty drawled. "You three would know about his share in this business with the pilgrims. That way, he'd never be safe. One day you'd get talking drunk and let out enough to interest people and there'd be plenty willing to listen. Even without you standing by and letting his son get crippled that's enough for him to want you dead."

"It's lies!" Gartree screeched. "All of it's lies!"

"You sent your hired gun after me," Dusty answered. "And your tame marshal to down him after he dropped me."

"Why—Why should I do a thing like that?" croaked the politician, his voice showing that Dusty guessed the truth.

"Could be the hired gun had a hold on you," Dusty explained. "He'd become an expensive nuisance. And it wouldn't do for folks to see a peace-loving jasper like you with that sort of regular company. So you told the marshal to kill him."

"Gruber'd never have the guts," Lanny commented.

"What risk was there?" countered Dusty. "The other feller would be busy watching and killing me. And the marshal stood well back with a scatter-gun. If the stakes were high enough, even he'd've got up enough nerve to chance that.''

"How about us?" growled Lanny, wanting information on the part of the affair which interested him the most.

"Try thinking, *hombre*," Dusty advised. "You *know* what would happen to you, especially yahoos like you three, if word got out in town that you'd mishandled and killed a woman.''

Once started thinking, Lanny and Coop needed no further aid to see their fate. After the way they had behaved in Bainesville for weeks, the citizens would need little stirring to paint for war; and the knowledge of the heinous crime the trio committed was more than enough to bring it about.

"But he'd be involved in it up to his slimy neck," Coop pointed out.

"Only who could prove it?" Dusty demanded.

"We could!''

"Sure you *could*—if you had the chance to talk and anybody believed you. Only you'd not get the chance. Gartree and his tame marshal'd see to that. It'd be Hickok-style, 'bang!' 'bang!' 'bang!' then call to you to halt when he was good and sure you couldn't do anything else but obey.''

While the two young men felt some pride in the achievements of Wild Bill Hickok, they reluctantly admitted that he did tend to shoot before challenging; and knew exactly what Dusty meant.

"Don't listen to him!" Gartree shrieked. "He can't prove a word he says.''

"I don't aim to try," Dusty answered. "All I'm going to do is make sure that you don't bother either me or them folks ahead any more.''

"Wh—What do you mean?"

"That white shirt makes a mighty handy mark. I figure that if I aim just about in the middle———"

"No!" Gartree screamed. "No———"

Turning, the politician flung himself wildly along the trail, running and swerving desperately. At any moment he expected to hear the carbine crack and feel lead rip into his body. Not even when he might have known himself out of any possible line of fire did he halt, but ran on through the night as if death stalked his flying feet.

"Looks like his important business could keep a mite longer," Dusty drawled.

"You never aimed to shoot him," Coop stated wonderingly.

"He thought that I did."

"Who are you, mister?" Lanny inquired.

"The name is Dusty Fog."

"Dusty Fog!"

Two young voices echoed the words. Interest and understanding showed in Coop and Lanny's voices as they realised how they came to meet defeat at the hands of such a small, insignificant-appearing man. Neither of them doubted Dusty's claim. In a way, it made them feel better to know the small Texan's identity. Nobody could blame them for losing out at the hands of the Rio Hondo gun wizard.

"What do you aim to do with us, Cap'n Fog?" asked Coop.

"Nothing."

"Nothing?" repeated two relieved voices.

"I figured you've learned some sense by now. Come ahead and collect your gear, then drift."

"Gee thanks, Cap'n," Lanny said.

"You reckon that Gartree meant to have us killed?" Coop asked as they came towards the tree.

"I reckon he did," Dusty replied.

"When we catch up with him, we ought to————"

"Leave him be," Dusty warned. "He's not worth it. Only, was I you, I'd not stick around Bainesville. He won't forget tonight and he's as mean as a teased diamondback."

"Know something," Lanny remarked, rasping a match on his pants' seat. "Ole Gartree allus kept telling us he's all for the working folk. After tonight, I reckon if he's for them, I'm sure happy that I never worked."

"Sure," agreed Coop. "Gavin was a snivelling, spineless rat most times, but alongside his pappy, he wasn't too bad."

Watching the young men locate and strap on their gunbelts, Dusty knew that he had done what he intended. Lanny and Coop had seen Gartree in his true colors and been given food for thought. It was highly unlikely that either would want to take further action against the travellers. Nor did Dusty expect trouble from the politician. Unless he misjudged Gartree's character, the man would keep on going and might even leave Bainesville for a safer location.

"I'm sorry about your horses," he told Lanny and Coop.

"Reckon a walk'll do us both good, Cap'n," Lanny replied. "And we sure as hell deserve it."

With that the two young men walked off down the trail. Dusty waited until the sound of their feet died away, then returned to his waiting paint. There was nothing to prevent him visiting the travellers' camp now.

CHAPTER NINE

The Travellers

Dusty kept his horse off the hard surface of the trail as he rode towards the clearing and its hooves made little sound on the springy turf under foot. For all that, he expected at least one of the strangers to have heard his approach. Folks travelling in the West tended to be alert and quick to catch even slight sounds at night. More so when having recently heard shooting.

Even when he rounded the final turn and came into plain sight of the clearing, the travellers gave no sign of being aware of his presence. They sat around a small wooden table, apparently at the end of a meal. To Dusty it seemed that the trio held a cheerful and interesting conversation, their whole attitude giving that impression, but their lips never moved and he heard no words.

While not a man easily swayed by impressions, Dusty felt just a touch perturbed by the silence of the trio. Even as Dusty watched, the young man looked at the girl like he was requesting something and, although no word passed, she handed him the sugar bowl.

Remembering the necessary etiquette, despite his uneasiness, Dusty halted the paint on the edge of the clearing and announced his presence.

"Hello the camp. Can I come on in?"

Dusty felt surprised at the casual manner in which the travellers accepted his appearance. Most folks would have displayed some agitation at suddenly hearing a voice and seeing a rider looming from out of the darkness. Even dudes fresh out from the East—or perhaps them more than most, for the blood and thunder novels of the day gave a graphic, if not entirely accurate, picture of the dangers and perils of the range country—usually showed more concern. Any party which had been as long on the trail as the trio must have, should know caution by now.

Instead of showing concern, the trio rose to their feet and turned towards Dusty. While the men's faces never lost their grave expression, they seemed amiable enough, and the girl smiled warmly at him.

"Come, please," said the elder man.

With permission granted, and not before, Dusty swung from the paint's saddle and walked forward. Although free, the stallion followed on his heels like a well trained hound-dog.

"Howdy, ma'am, gents," he greeted.

"Good evening," replied the elder man and the younger nodded.

"Mind if I share your fire for the night, sir?"

"Of course not. Vaza, lay out a meal for our guest."

"Don't go to any trouble, ma'am," Dusty told the girl. "I've———"

"But it is no trouble," smiled the girl. "Please come and sit at the table while I prepare something."

The younger man flashed a glance at the girl, almost as if objecting to her suggestion and an embarrassed expression flickered across her expressive face. Yet the man displayed no hostility to Dusty and raised no objections to accepting the small Texan as a guest.

"Perhaps you would wish to care for your horse," the elder man suggested. "Vaza can prepare your meal while you do so."

"I was just going to say that, sir," Dusty replied, noticing the relief that flickered on the younger man's face. "But if it'll put you———"

"I can easily prepare food for you," the girl, to whom Dusty's last words had been directed, replied.

"If you require any help, I will come with you," the younger man went on.

"Thanks, but I can handle him better alone," Dusty answered, puzzled by the other's friendly offer and earlier conduct.

Turning, Dusty took the paint's reins and led it across the clearing in the direction of the stream. Not until after he had removed the bit and allowed his horse to lower its head towards the clear waters did he realise that no questions had been asked about the shooting. Possibly the wind, blowing from the direction of the camp, and the thickness of the trees helped blanket the sound, but the travellers ought to have heard enough to arouse their interest if nothing more. He sensed their eyes on him and expected that at any moment one or another would come over and ask questions. Time passed, the horse drank its fill and still the expected questions never came. Then Dusty realised that none of the trio spoke even among themselves, after he walked away from them.

With the horse satisfied, Dusty took it closer to the wagon. Stripping off the saddle and blanket, he stood back and allowed the horse to indulge in a good roll on the ground. He spent the time in opening his bedroll and extracting the set of hobbles from the top of his warbag.

While Dusty could trust the paint not to roam too far, he knew its nature too well to leave it free in the presence of strange horses.

Unnoticed by Dusty, the girl crossed the clearing, leaving her cooking pot steaming on the fire, and walked towards him. On completing its roll, the horse lurched to its feet and stood patiently waiting for the nightly ritual its master always followed. Before offering to feed the horse, Dusty checked on its general condition and examined its shoes. The fact that he looked at the near hind leg first did not imply lack of faith in Morley's work, but came about because Dusty happened to be closest to that leg when starting his examination. Checking the horse's shoes at the end of a day's work came naturally to Dusty. Such small details could mean the difference between life and death to a man who rode dangerous trails and so might at any time need the unrestricted speed that only a well-shod horse could give him.

Hearing the paint's explosive warning snort, Dusty glanced up. He saw the girl approaching and did not need to observe the horse's laid-back ears and flaring nostrils to become aware of her danger. Well-trained the paint might be, but it was still a spirited stallion and did not take kindly to strangers approaching too close.

The girl halted just beyond the reach of the paint's jaws and stood looking directly at it. Tensing for a spring, and hoping he would be in time to save Vaza from an attack, Dusty became aware of a change in the paint's behavior. Although the girl never spoke, the big horse relaxed; its ears came erect and the angry snort died off. Walking closer, the girl laid her hand on the horse's neck and it lowered its head to gently nuzzle at the front of her dress.

"This is a fine animal," she said. "Did you have its shoe—replaced?"

"Yes, ma'am," Dusty replied, trying to hide his relief; and a trifle puzzled at the paint's unusual docility.

"Why were you so worried when I came here?"

"I thought you might get hurt. Was I you, I'd not make a habit of going up to a strange horse like that."

"Why not?"

"Like I said, you could get hurt. Some horses, including that one of mine, don't take to strangers handling them. Although I reckon he showed mighty good taste this time."

It seemed that Vaza did not understand Dusty's compliment at first. A gentle frown creased her brow; then it died away and she smiled once more. Her eyes went to the hobbles in Dusty's hand and she showed some interest as he knelt down to fix them in place.

"Why do you do that?" she asked, watching him buckle one cuff of the hobbles to each of the paint's forelegs.

"I don't want this ornery cuss going over and starting a fight with your stock in the night."

"Couldn't you—— No. I suppose not. I can see how it restricts the horse's movements. It is a good idea. We never thought of it."

"How'd you fasten your horses at nights then?"

"We haven't needed—— Come and look."

"I'll just finish him off first," Dusty replied.

"Oh!" the girl gasped. "Your meal. I will go and attend to it. Perhaps you will show Jarrel these——"

"We call them hobbles," Dusty explained, guessing that she did not know the English word, but mildly puzzled at her failing to recognise such familiar objects.

"He will be most interested, for he was saying earlier

that he thought our way of securing the horses was inadequate.''

"I'll take a look," Dusty promised and lifted a nose-bag from out of his bedroll. "Just let me feed my horse first."

"Speaking of food," Vaza said. "I'd better go and see to your meal."

"I don't want to put you to any trouble, Miss————"

"You may call me 'Vaza'," the girl smiled.

"Thank you, ma'am. I'd like some hot water so that I can clean my guns when I've fed."

"I will have some waiting for you."

With that the girl walked away. Dusty strapped the paint's feed bag in place and watched his horse commence feeding. A low chuckle left Dusty's lips and he warned the horse that there would be no more grain-feeding until they came to the next town.

"Does he understand you?" asked the younger man, coming up.

"If he does, he's sure tolerant, some of the things I've called him at times," Dusty replied. "It gets to be a habit, talking to your horse, when you ride alone for a spell."

"Then you haven't found a way to communicate with animals?"

"Not so's we can sit down and talk about the weather."

"We haven't advanced to that stage ourselves yet. Vaza tells me that you have an interesting manner of securing your horse."

"Don't you use hobbles back in your old country?" asked Dusty.

"No. May I look?"

"Feel free. Just let me hold his head."

Bending down, the younger of the strangers examined

the hobbles with interest. "Interesting," he said.

"How do you hold your horses?" asked Dusty.

"We have no need, they do not run away."

"That's a chance I'd rather not take," Dusty drawled. "Especially in wooded country. Happen a cougar spooks them, you'll never get them back again."

"Spooks?"

"Frightens them so that they run away. It's none of my affair, but I'd fasten them and move them closer to the fire before you go to bed. They'll let you know if they catch cat scent and you can soon scare the cougar away. Mind if I look your stock over."

"As you would say, feel free."

While walking towards the four team horses, Dusty studied the man at his side. He found it hard to gauge the other's age. The beard and face seemed to be that of a man in his late middle-age, yet he walked as spry as a youngster and had a fairly powerful frame under the sober suit. Nor could Dusty form any conclusion about the relationship of the man and girl. There did not seem to be any family likeness between them, for he was dark haired and the girl fair.

Putting aside his thoughts on the humans, Dusty turned his attention to the horses. The first thing to catch his eye was that, although ideally built for haulage work, the animals did not appear to belong to any breed with which he had become familiar. Strong, powerful, well developed for pulling a heavy wagon, the four horses stood free, their feed bags in place; although not in a manner which met with Dusty's approval.

"What is wrong with the nose-bags?" asked Jarrel.

"You haven't strapped them up tight enough," Dusty replied. "Hanging loose like that, the horse can't touch the food in the bottom and starts tossing its head trying to reach it, spills most of it."

Not until he stopped speaking did Dusty wonder how the other knew what he thought about the set of the nose-bags. Before he could mention the fact, Dusty saw Jarrel step forward and make the necessary adjustments.

After the horses had fed on the grain, Dusty helped remove the nose-bags and showed Jarrel how to turn them inside out to facilitate drying. Then they took the animals closer to the campfire and he improvised hobbles from rope. By which time the girl announced that the food was ready.

"Thanks, ma'am," he said, walking towards the table. "Reckon we'd best get acquainted. I'm sorry for not doing it before."

While not an egoist, Dusty felt mildly surprised at the lack of response to his name. His fame had spread far over the Western ranges and even extended to the East, where highly colored stories of his adventures occasionally appeared in the *Police Gazette* and *New York Ledger*. Consequently many dudes reacted to hearing his name, but the trio showed no sign that it meant anything to them.

"We are pleased to know you, Mr. Fog," said the elder man.

"I've never been one for 'mister-ing'," Dusty replied. "If it's all one with you, I'd rather you said 'Dusty'."

"Dusty?" repeated the girl, looking puzzled.

"It's short for Dustine. I was called that after my uncle. But it's a mite too long to be yelled in a hurry, so it was shortened to 'Dusty'."

"I see," she smiled.

"I am Adek," the elder man introduced. "This is Jarrel and Vaza."

"Right pleased to know all of you," Dusty answered.

"And now you must eat," Vaza told him.

"We must attend to our chores, Jarrel," Adek remarked. "Come."

At the table a surprise awaited Dusty. Instead of the stew he expected, a plate of boiled potatoes, peas, beef and gravy met his gaze.

"It is all right?" the girl asked.

"It sure is," agreed Dusty and wondered how she managed to produce such a meal when using only one pan.

"Then eat, please."

Dusty's surprise did not end as he sat down and started to eat. On taking up his knife to cut the beef, he found the task considerably easier than usual. While the Texas longhorn possessed many sterling qualities, Dusty was the first to admit that its meat left much to be desired. Often he and his uncle had discussed the possibility and advisability of trying to introduce a new strain of cattle, one giving better beef, to the range; but could not think of another breed capable of living the half-wild existence of the longhorn.

The meat into which Dusty cut did not come from any longhorn, of that he felt sure. Yet it could hardly be any other kind. Sure, there were beef strains in the East, but not in any quantity; which explained why the longhorn, bred in vast numbers on the open ranges of the west, found such a ready sale that the expense of trying to introduce a better meat strain did not justify itself.

Tasting the meat, Dusty knew it to be beef and not the flesh of deer, wapiti, buffalo, antelope or any other wild animal. Yet it did not seem possible that the trio could have brought meat and kept it fresh, all the way from the East.

"I hope it is satisfactory," Vaza remarked after Dusty had been eating for a short time.

"It sure is, Miss Vaza," he answered. "This's mighty

good beef. Did you buy it on the trail?"

"No. We brought it with us," she replied and poured out a cup of coffee.

Raised in a land where one did not question others too closely, Dusty did not ask if she understood his questions, or inquire how the travellers managed to keep their meat fresh during the long train journey West and during their wagon trip from the railroad town at which they arrived.

"Adek wondered about getting more fuel for the fire," she said. "We found sufficient for our needs by the place where we made our fire."

"Don't you carry any in the possum-belly of your wagon?" asked Dusty.

"Possum-belly, what is that?"

Turning, Dusty looked towards the wagon, directing his glance underneath but not seeing the sheet of rawhide usually fastened there to act as a repository for firewood. He explained to the girl what he meant and she nodded.

"Of course. Possum is short for opossum and that is a marsupial, carrying its young in a pouch under its belly. Oh, I would love to see one. Are there any in this area?"

"Maybe. I don't know much about this section of Kansas. We have plenty of them down home, but the only time we see them is when we're running the hounds at night after coon. About that wood———?"

"Adek and Jarrel are already attending to gathering more," Vaza replied.

Dusty swung his head from looking at the wagon and saw the two men walking off into the trees. Then he glanced at the girl. She had removed the sun-bonnet and golden blonde hair framed her face, hanging shoulder long.

Thinking of the girl's lack of knowledge, he put it down to her not speaking English as a native tongue. Yet he found himself hard-pressed to guess at what her language might be, not having heard her, or her companions, speak anything but English. All the trio looked Anglo-Saxon in their features, but their names did not sound English. Nor did they strike Dusty as being Norwegian, Dutch, German or belonging to any of the other North European nations. Range etiquette did not allow the asking of direct questions, but Dusty figured that he would satisfy his curiosity before leaving the party.

"Do you folks have any guns?" he asked, suddenly realising that he had seen no weapons around the camp.

"Of course not. We are peace-loving people."

"So am I," Dusty replied.

"But you go armed," Vaza objected.

"Yes, ma'am. That's so that other folks respect my wanting."

"I don't understand."

"Look at it this way," Dusty explained. "A cougar will jump a whole herd of doe whitetails—whitetail deer—and kill them all, because they've no way of fighting back. But he'll think long before he tried it on a big old buck with a hatrack head of horns."

"Hatrack?"

"Take a set of buck's horns and hang them on the wall, and you've pegs for visitors to hang their hats on."

"You must think me terribly silly not knowing such things."

"No," Dusty answered. "You're just not used to speaking English, I reckon."

"That is true. But your ideas about the cougar do not meet my argument. I can't quite follow them."

"The best way to live in peace is to make good and

sure that you've something around to defend yourself against folks who don't want to leave you peaceable. The whitetail buck's got horns for that.''

"But animals and human beings are different.''

"There are times, and folk, that make me think there's no difference,'' Dusty replied.

"You mean those men in the town we visited?'' asked Vaza. "Did you have any further trouble with them?''

"Nothing to talk about.''

"Who were they and why did they act like they did?''

"I never learned their names, but I've seen their kind around almost every big town. Lord knows why they do things, just ornery I guess. I hope they didn't scare you too much, Miss Vaza.''

"I was afraid,'' the girl admitted. "I thought that I could communicate with them, but it did not work.''

"The best way to communicate with that sort is from behind a ten gauge shotgun,'' Dusty drawled. "And talking of guns, I'd like to clean mine.''

"There is water in the pan,'' the girl replied and looked to where her two companions returned, each carrying a good pile of wood.

Having finished his meal while talking, Dusty left the table. Not until he stood by the fire and looked into the pan full of hot water did he realise that the girl had not taken it out of his sight or washed it, yet it showed no signs of being used for cooking his meal.

CHAPTER TEN

Mighty Strong Iron

"May I watch you?" asked Jarrel, dropping the pile of wood he carried and walking to where Dusty stood unbuckling the gunbelt ready to clean his weapons.

"It's your camp," Dusty replied. "Do you know much about guns?"

"Only the general principle of how they work."

"Like I just told Miss Vaza, I'd sure get at least one was I you."

With that, Dusty collected his saddle and brought it to the side of the fire. Taking his cleaning gear from the warbag, he asked for and was granted permission to use the table while working.

"You would advise us to obtain weapons?" Adek inquired. "What kind is best?"

"Every man to his own taste, but I figure the Army Colt's about as good a revolver as you can buy," Dusty answered, deftly stripping the gun he used to defend himself against Latter and the marshal.

"It appears to be a simple mechanism," Jarrel commented, watching the removal of the few screws which allowed the Colt's works to be stripped.

"Simple and sure," agreed Dusty. "Trust old Colonel Sam's boys for that."

"Colonel Sam?"

"Colonel Samuel Colt. He died back in '62, but his company keep up the standard he started. Doesn't he sell arms in your old country?"

"No."

"Happen he knew that, he'd take the first boat there. My Uncle Devil's told me about Colonel Sam, reckoned he was some salesman. When I said he'd take the first boat, I meant he would while he was alive. His boys from the Hartford factory don't miss many bets in that line either. I'm surprised that none of them have been to your country."

"The journey would be too difficult," smiled Adek. "Is the other weapon also made by the Colt factory?"

"The carbine?" Dusty said, surprised that anybody should express such ignorance. "No. That's a Winchester, which's to rifle companies what Colt is to the handgun makers."

"May I examine it?" asked Jarrel.

"Reckon I'd best unload it first," Dusty answered. "I have to clean it."

"We have so much to learn," Vaza remarked. "Of course, we were not meant to come, but the———"

She stopped abruptly, her face swinging towards Adek. To Dusty it seemed almost as if the man gave some unseen signal which prevented the girl from going any further. Clearly Adek did not want too much saying about his party's presence in the country. Being a man who could respect another's wishes, Dusty did not press for information. After cleaning his Colts, he unloaded the Winchester, explained its mechanism to Jarrel and gave it a thorough cleaning.

"I reckon I'll turn in," Dusty remarked after finishing the cleaning and reloading the carbine.

"And so will we," Adek replied. "Where will you sleep?"

"By the fire."

"In the open?" gasped the girl.

"I spend more nights that way than in my bed," grinned Dusty. "Don't worry none about me, I'll be all right. It's a fine night."

"I suppose it is," agreed the girl and looked up at the star-dotted sky. "I wish you good night, Dusty."

"Good night, Miss Vaza."

After the girl walked to the wagon and disappeared inside, Dusty spread his bedroll out. The two men said their good nights and walked to the wagon, also entering. A few moments later, just as Dusty was thinking that they would be unlikely to share the inside with the girl, they emerged carrying blankets and made their beds under the wagon. Collecting his paint, Dusty led it closer to the fire. He dropped a couple of logs on to the dying blaze and then stretched out on his bed. With the gunbelt under the blankets and his carbine resting against the saddle he used for the pillow, Dusty settled down to sleep. Before dropping off, Dusty gave some thought to his companions and wondered who they were, where they came from, but could reach no decision. Still pondering on which European country might be so difficult to reach that the far-travelling salesmen of the Colt or Winchester companies failed to find it, Dusty went to sleep.

A snort from the paint woke Dusty. Twisting around in his blankets, he found that the fire had died down somewhat, but it still gave out enough light for him to see all he needed. He read a certain significance in the way his horse rose to its feet, extending its neck and shaking its head as it looked across the clearing. Even as he followed the direction in which the horse stared,

Dusty reached for the waiting carbine. He knew just
what he would see, and did not need to hear the low
grating snarl which came to his ears to understand what
disturbed the paint.

Just at the edge of the fire's flickering glare, devil's
face twisted in a snarl which showed the long canine
teeth, body crouched with rippling muscles tensed for a
spring, long tail lashing from side to side, was one of the
large, pale fawn, short-coated cougars common to the
Great Plains country of the North-Central United
States. The cougar must have been a young tom, Dusty
judged from its size and the fact that it committed the
folly of making its stalk on the camp with the wind at its
back. Now it crouched and tried to gather sufficient
courage to make a charge through the firelight and at
the horse.

Thoughts tore through Dusty's head. He knew his
skill with the carbine, but did not wish to cut loose on
the cougar unless sure his first bullet would kill. While
a cougar could not be classed with the jaguar—which
occasionally came over the Rio Grande and into Dusty's
home country—in the danger line, one wounded was
unpredictable. It might run, or just as easily make a
determined charge. Tangling with a wounded, two hundred and twenty pound cougar was not Dusty's idea of a
pastime. Yet he knew he must do something—and fast
—before all the horses spooked to hell-and-gone, injur-
ing themselves badly in their attempts at flight while
hobbled.

"Yeeagh!"

Letting out as blood-thirsty a rebel war screech as he
ever managed when raiding a Yankee camp during the
War, Dusty thrust himself from his bed. He whipped
the carbine to his shoulder as he rose, ready to shoot
should it become necessary, and hoping that the Great

Plains cougar reacted in the same manner as the very large, greyish variety he knew from back home in Texas.

Fast though Dusty moved, he still had the carbine only half raised when there was no further need for it. Turning in a single fluid motion, the cougar took off in a long bound which carried it away from the light and into the welcome blackness beyond. Just one crash told of its arrival among the bushes, a brief rustling, then silence.

Lowering his carbine, Dusty went towards the paint. Swiftly and gently he calmed his horse and directed a glance towards the travellers' wagon team. Much to his surprise, he saw that not one of the four animals showed the slightest concern or fear; even though they, like the paint, must have caught the cougar's scent as it stalked them.

"Is something wrong, Dusty?" asked Adek, peering from under the wagon.

"A cougar came, but it's gone now."

"Did you say a cougar?" called Vaza, her tousled little head appearing at the end of the wagon.

"Sure," agreed Dusty. "I've frightened it away."

"Oh, why, Dusty? I would have so liked to study it."

"Likely," he grinned. "Only it was fixing to study our horses. I figured that my need was greater than his."

"I suppose so," the girl smiled back. "There is no chance that the cougar will return?"

"Happen he does," Dusty growled, "I'll make sure that you get a chance to study him real close."

With that Dusty prepared to go back to bed. First he made up the fire, piling the wood carefully to give the maximum length of burning time. Then he made a circle of the area so as to leave his scent around. Few predatory animals in a reasonably civilised area would come too close to the hated scent of human beings. A glance towards the paint told him that the scare had left it and it was settling down again, while the four team horses still showed the stolid unconcern which so puzzled him. After a final word of reassurance to the travellers, Dusty went to his bed and slid between the blankets to return to sleep.

Dawn came without further incident or return of the cougar. Dusty woke and stirred in his blankets, thinking wistfully of daybreak with the trail herd. Already the cook would have built up the fire and there would be coffee bubbling in the pot for the awakening crew. Under the present conditions, he knew that he must rise, build up the fire and wait until water heated before being able to take a hot drink.

Automatically his eyes swept the camp, finding nothing to disturb him. The horses stood grazing and seemed to be in good health. None of the travellers had made an appearance yet, so Dusty rose. He made up the fire and carried the coffeepot to the stream, tipping its contents away, rinsing it out and filling it with clean water.

"Good morning, Dusty," said a voice as he returned to the fire and set the coffee-pot on the edge of the flames.

"Morning, Adek," he replied. "How'd you sleep?"

"Very well considering that I am unused to doing so on the ground."

Dusty wondered where the old man had slept on the previous nights of their journey, for it seemed unlikely that they managed their route so as to end each day in a town. Before he could satisfy his curiosity, he saw Vaza swing lithely down from the wagon. Clad in the same gingham dress, she left off her sun-bonnet and golden blonde hair framed her beautiful face. Dusty

thought that discarding the hat was an improvement
and admired the graceful manner in which she moved,
for she showed a remarkable agility in leaving the
wagon.

"Good morning, Dusty," she greeted. "Thank you
for fetching the water. I will cook breakfast while you
attend to your horse."

"That'd be best," he replied. "You wouldn't like my
cooking; I know I don't."

Leaving the girl to her chores, Dusty went across to
his paint. He unbuckled the hobbles, muttering a grim
warning of what he would do happen the horse caused
fuss with the wagon team, and allowed the big stallion
to go to the stream. By now it ought to have become
accustomed in some measure to the other animals and
less likely to want to try conclusions. Turning, Dusty
found that the two men were with their horses and went
to help them.

Speaking gently, he approached one of the team from
the side and, when sure he had gained the animal's confidence, bent to remove the hobbles. With that done, he
began to check on the horse's feet. Although he expected some resistance to his handling, the horse gave
none, but allowed him to raise the foot he gripped.

Something of a surprise awaited Dusty. He expected
to see the usual misguided care; a neatly dumped foot
with smoothly pared sole, heels opened out, frog
trimmed to a symmetrical neatness. Instead he looked
down at a strong, natural, although rougher-looking
hoof, its sole appearing flaky and frog large and ragged.
In view of the current line of thought on horses' feet,
Dusty wondered where they found a blacksmith enlight-
ened enough to know the insidious nature of the 'im-
provements' perpetrated as normal practice.

Such was Dusty's interest in the natural condition of

the foot, that the shoe did not attract his attention for a few seconds and he failed to grasp the significance of what he saw immediately.

In every respect the shoe appeared to be normal enough with plenty of cover from the web, calks raised on the toe and heel as one might expect in a draught animal that required something to give a firmer grip on the ground when starting or taking a load up a slope.

However, Dusty felt puzzled as he looked down. The shoe appeared to have been placed on recently, for it showed no sign of wear, not even on its calks—and this after at least a hundred miles of travel from the last place where they could have found a blacksmith.

On checking, Dusty found that all the shoes showed the same remarkable state of preservation. By the time he had finished, Jarrel came to his side.

"Is all well, Dusty?"

"It sure is. That's mighty tough iron you use for shoeing though."

"It is."

"I see you folks don't go for paring the sole or trimming the frog."

For a moment Jarrel did not reply as if he appeared to be translating the English terms into his own language. Then he nodded gravely. "We have found that it is best left so."

"And me," Dusty admitted. "Did you find any trouble in persuading a blacksmith that it's best?"

"No, of course not."

"You sure had luck. I usually have to force the issue when I'm on the trail. Down home, my uncle's the smith and I'm lucky, he agrees with me. Fact being, it was him who first showed me about the damage all the paring does to the horse's foot."

"He was a discerning man."

"Sure, but there aren't many like him about."

"We have no need to concern ourselves on that score," Jarrel stated. "Our team was shod before we left home and will last us for our journey."

"Breakfast is ready," called Vaza from the fire, preventing Dusty from asking how shoes put on in Europe could still look so new, or inquiring how much longer the travellers would be moving before they reached their destination.

"Come," Jarrel said, smiling. "Vaza does not like to be kept waiting."

"I've yet to meet the woman who does," Dusty replied, feeling a little annoyed by the smile. It almost seemed that Jarrel read his thoughts, enjoyed his puzzlement, but wished to keep him from raising the matter.

In the range country a man did not pursue a conversation when shown that the other party wanted it dropping, so Dusty said no more. Yet the hardness of the iron and the almost unbelievable lasting qualities of the shoes added another mystery to those already surrounding his companions.

"You go and eat, Dusty," Adek suggested. "Jarrel and I will ready our wagon for moving."

"Is there anything I can do?" Dusty asked.

"I think not. Besides, Vaza would like a chance to talk with somebody other than we two."

Came to a point, Dusty could not think of a single objection to finding a chance to speak with the girl—not that he tried very hard. Leaving the horses grazing, he walked over to where Vaza set plates on the table. Breakfast consisted of ham and eggs, with more of the excellent coffee the girl brewed. Dusty gave up trying to think how the girl turned out meals of surprising quality over a wood fire and using the simplest methods.

After discussing the cougar's visit, with the girl

showing a lively interest and some knowledge of the animal's habits, Dusty found himself looking forward to travelling in the company of the trio for a time and wondered how he might suggest it without risking giving offence.

"We would be pleased for you to accompany us," the girl remarked.

Only by exercising all his will-power did Dusty avoid letting his surprise show. For the second time in a very short period it seemed that one of the travellers could read his thoughts.

"Well," he said. "I like company and hate riding alone————"

"And we need somebody to look after us," Vaza smiled.

Again the girl appeared to have followed his line of thought, for he had been concerned over their lack of armament and horse-savvy.

"I wouldn't have put it that way," he told her.

"Of course not, you are too polite."

"You wouldn't want to put that in writing, would you?" Dusty grinned.

"Why?" asked Vaza, sounding startled.

"So that I can show it to my trail crew next time we meet up."

A puzzled expression came to the girl's face, puckering her brow in an attractive manner. At last she shook her head and turned her luminous eyes to Dusty.

"I am afraid that I do not understand you."

"It was a joke—and not a very good one."

"Could you explain it?"

"Well, a trail boss doesn't have time to be polite— and rarely has the inclination when he's concerned with trailing a herd of around three thousand head of ornery, mean-minded long-horns north to the railroad."

"Longhorns?"

"Texas longhorn cattle. Just about the most awkward, vicious, cross-grained critters the Good Lord ever made. Comes to a point, we didn't start the breed, but took it over from the Mexicans along with the country."

"You must excuse my ignorance," the girl warned. "You see, I am a naturalist, but know so little about your wor—country. That is why I came, to study the animal life. So if I ask many questions———"

"It will be my pleasure to answer them, ma'am," Dusty replied soberly, but the twinkle in his eyes brought a merry smile to her face. "Do you mind if I ask a few in return?"

"It will be *my* pleasure to answer them, sir," Vaza countered.

While talking, Dusty watched the men. Although they handled their work competently, neither seemed as adept at it as might be expected. He noticed that they omitted several small, but important details in their preparation for the day's travel.

"Adek and Jarrel do not do their work properly, you think, Dusty?" asked the girl.

"I didn't reckon it showed," he answered.

"But you———" she began, stopped and shook her head. "I guessed it from the way you looked."

"I'll never play poker again," Dusty said. "Did you lose your driver?"

"There was a slight accident and the party who should have come met with injury. That is why we came. I was the only naturalist aboard, so had to come; although I am not experienced."

"Then you're not members of a religious sect travelling to join your people?"

"Oh, no. Why did you think that?" Vaza replied. "The young man in Bainesville had the same idea."

"It's the clothes you wear," Dusty explained. "Mostly Quakers, some Mormons and members of other small religious groups dress that way."

"I see. And do people object to such groups?"

"In some places. Those bunch back in Bainesville weren't worried about what religion you follow, they just wanted to raise fuss."

"And you?" smiled the girl. "Do you object to people who don't follow your beliefs?"

"Way I see it, a man's free to believe what he wants and worship how he wants; as long as he doesn't try to force his ways on me."

"You are a tolerant man, Dusty."

"Like I said, there're some who'd give you an argument on that."

"Well, we have no connection with any religious group. Our purpose here is purely scientific. We came to study your wor—country."

"Do you always travel with Adek?" asked Dusty.

"No. This is the first time we've been on an expedition together."

"Are he and Jarrel your kin-folk—father and brother, I mean."

A smile flickered across the girl's face. "They are not related to me. Adek is a historian and Jarrel an engineer. We were sent to see how your country has advanced and developed since our last party made a visit."

"Did they settle in the United States?"

"No," the girl replied. "It is not our desire or intention to settle, merely to study and learn. Unfortunately three out of four of the last party were killed on their expedition."

"By Indians?" Dusty inquired, suggesting the most likely cause of the tragedy.

"No. The one who escaped brought the story of what happened. Naturally our ways appeared strange to your people and the party found themselves accused of witchcraft. Three were killed in a horrible manner."

"Where'd this happen?"

"In a town called Salem."

Thinking back to half-forgotten history lessons while at school, Dusty remembered how the town of Salem in Massachusetts had been the scene of mass accusations of witchcraft. A number of people were tried as witches and several killed before the Governor of the Colony— as it was then—intervened and brought an end to the burning at the stake and hanging. While Dusty could not recall the exact date, he decided that the affair took place in the late seventeenth century.*

"And none of your people have been back since then?" he asked.

"Not to the United States," Vaza replied. "It was decided that we direct our attentions to other parts of your world, although we have kept observations on the happenings here. At last it was decided that another party landed. There was, as I told you, an accident and the selected party could not come. Rather than cancel the expedition after so much effort, Adek, Jarrel and myself were sent."

"You know something," smiled Dusty, putting the girl's reference to 'your world' down to a faulty knowledge of English grammar. "I'm right pleased, for one, that you came."

"Why?" asked Vaza.

At that moment Adek and Jarrel returned, so Dusty put off explaining the reasons for his pleasure until a more suitable time. Running a hand across the beard

---

* The date was 1692.

stubble on his cheeks, he decided that he would remove it.

"I reckon that I'll go wash and shave," he remarked.

"Very well," Adek replied. "We will make our preparations for departure and be ready to start when you return."

CHAPTER ELEVEN

The Customs of the Country

Leaving the camp, Dusty passed through the bushes in the direction of the stream and halted out of sight of the wagon. Placing his towel handy, he set up the small, polished steel mirror, which he carried on the trail, upon a suitable branch of a near-by bush. Instinct caused him to retain his gunbelt. Not that he felt he would need it; but because if the need should arise, there would be no time to start running back to the wagon to collect it. Peeling off his shirt, he took up the bar of soap and was about to start washing when he heard a rustling in the bushes.

On turning, Dusty saw Vaza coming towards him. He removed his right hand from the butt of the left side Colt and started to raise the towel before him. Embarrassment at his small size did not cause the move. With his shirt removed, his powerful development showed fully and had the Coopers or Lanny been present to study his muscular frame, they would have understood better how he came to handle them with such apparent ease. Dusty had nothing to be ashamed of as far as a manly well-developed body went. Born and raised in the strict traditions of a Southern gentleman, although he rarely found use on the trail for the social graces his mother struggled to instil, Dusty had strict views on the way he should act around women. In the late 1870's, a man did not allow a presentable young woman to see him stripped to the waist.

The girl showed no embarrassment as she approached, carrying a towel and soap in one hand. Even as Dusty opened his mouth to speak, he received a shock which momentarily jolted the words out of his mouth. Vaza's dress fastened down the front to waist level and she began to unbutton it. Even so that might not have been so bad if she wore the kind of underwear one expected a young lady of her class to use. Under her dress she had nothing and opening it exposed more and more of her firm white flesh to Dusty's amazed gaze.

Cohesive thought returned to Dusty as Vaza slipped one arm free of the dress and her round breasts came into view. He felt his cheeks burn and knew they must be very red under the tan. Swiftly he turned away from the girl, sensing her coming close behind him.

"Am I doing wrong, Dusty?" she asked, halting and appearing to follow his thoughts again. "I only wish to wash before we commence the journey."

"That figures," Dusty replied. "But not that way."

"But I only do as you do."

"That'd be fine if we were both girls," Dusty explained, not turning and trying to pick the right words.

"But what has that to do with our washing?"

"I don't know how it is in your country," Dusty answered, "but over here a young lady doesn't undress in front of a man unless they're married."

"Oh, I see," the girl said, sounding puzzled. Then she gave a shrug. "We are always told to adhere to the customs of the country. I will find another place for my wash."

"It'd be best," Dusty breathed.

"You need not feel embarrassed. In my wor—country, we have no such inhibitions about undressing and washing together."

"I bet the boys enjoy that," Dusty remarked, trying to smooth the incident over and introduce a lighter note.

"Why should they———" Vaza began. "You were joking, of course."

"I tried to," Dusty admitted.

"When training for the expedition, I was told that often understanding another people's sense of humor was the hardest part of passing among them. But I delay you, Dusty. If you wish to continue your ablutions, I will find another place and make mine."

With a feeling of relief, Dusty heard the girl walk away and resumed his interrupted wash. During the time he took to lather up and shave, Dusty thought of the girl's actions and found they added yet another puzzling facet to the mystery surrounding the trio of travellers. While aware that moral standards differed from country to country, he could not recall having heard of one in which the young men and women were allowed sufficient licence as to strip and wash in each other's presence. Of course, one did hear stories about the behavior of people in France; but, after knowing a number of French people, Dusty discounted most of what he heard.

Another point in his train of thought followed from his views on the French. At the time of the Salem witch trials, only Britain, France and Holland had gained a foothold on the North American continent; the Spanish concentrating their efforts farther south. Vaza did not come from any of those countries, of that Dusty felt sure. All could be reached with ease, and had regularly supplied the growing United States with immigrants; as well as being regularly visited by Colt and Winchester salesmen.

Dusty had still reached no decision on the matter when he returned to the clearing. Finding the others ready to move out, he wasted no time in asking questions, but packed his bedroll and saddled the paint ready to move out.

Riding alongside the wagon, Dusty found the girl interested in everything she saw. Vaza sat on the outside of the trio, her face alight with delight and eyes glowing at every sight of wild animals no matter what their size. To her, a mouse scuttling across the trail held as much interest as did the sight of a magnificent bull elk which halted on a rim, its great antlered head thrown back in lofty defiance as it watched the wagon roll by.

Questions flowed from the girl and Dusty found himself hard-pressed to answer some of them, especially about the smaller creatures which rarely if ever attracted his attention. He told her what he could and found Vaza just as interested in the cattle-raising business as in his repeating the old Indian legend that a red-skin hunter would apologise to a black bear before killing it with a club; the black bear being regarded by the brave-heart warriors as harmless and not worthy of a death blow by arrow or war lance.

"Mind you," Dusty continued. "I've never tried clubbing one, or met an Indian who had. But the legend's repeated."

"I have always found that legends are based on fact, slight though the basis may be in some cases, Dusty," Adek put in. "You have the story of the boy who cried 'Wolf!'?"

"Sure."

"I have heard the same story repeated by natives of the Indian continent, but with the tiger as the warning;

and also in Africa where the boy cried 'lion'.''

"But why did the Indians wish to kill the bear?" asked Vaza.

"For food, its skin made a fine blanket too," Dusty explained. "They hadn't come to shooting for sport—although a bear's skin made a mighty fine show to the little Indian girls.''

So engrossed had Dusty been in the conversation that he lost all idea of the passage of time. A glance at the sky handed him something of a shock, for he found the time to be almost noon. Soon after the party found a stream on the banks of which they halted. After caring for the horses, the men ate a cold meal that Vaza prepared. Much as Dusty wanted to bring up some of the puzzling aspects of his companions' presence, he found no opportunity and was still as much in the dark as ever when they moved on again.

A couple of miles from the stream, Dusty saw something and made what to him was an automatic reaction. Halting in its tracks, a Great Plains buffalo wolf, medium-sized, light buff pelage grizzled with black, head short, broad and powerful, gave the wagon and rider a suspicious stare. Reaching down, Dusty slid the carbine from its boot and started to raise it. Realising its danger, the wolf turned and darted swiftly away. While the wolf stayed in sight for some considerable distance, Dusty did not fire. His carbine's rear sight had graduations for shooting up to three hundred yards; but he knew that the combination of a short barrel and weak powder charge did not make for accuracy at any but short distances. Not wishing to waste lead by missing, or, worse still, wound the wolf, Dusty held his fire and watched the animal fade into the distance.

"Why did you do that, Dusty?" asked Vaza in a disapproving tone.

"I reckon it's a cattleman's instincts," he replied.

"The wolf was doing no wrong."

"Not right now," admitted Dusty. "But I've seen what a pack can do to a herd of cattle, especially at calf-down time."

"The wolf serves a very useful purpose," Vaza insisted.

"I don't see how."

"Its hunting helps break up and scatter the herd of grass-eating animals and ensure that new blood is introduced which prevents in-breeding among them. This in turn serves to keep the strain healthy."

"Maybe," Dusty drawled. "But, like I said, I'm a cattleman and spend enough time now trying to prevent my spreads stock scattering. I can do without wolves chasing the cattle around, running beef off them and killing off saleable stock."

"You will find yourself in disagreement with Vaza, Dusty," Jarrel warned with a grin. "She is a zoologist who believes that all animals have the right to exist."

"I'm not going to argue on that," Dusty grinned back. "What kind of animals do you want to study, Vaza?"

"All kinds," the girl answered.

"Do you want for me to shoot any for you?"

"No! Why should I?"

"I thought that you scientific folks always wanted specimens to examine," Dusty told her and slid the carbine into its boot. "We've had a couple come from back east to visit the ranch and always had to hunt down some critter they wanted to study."

"I can assure you that I do not work that way!" Vaza snorted.

"It is not our policy on these expeditions to destroy any creature to further our studies, Dusty," Adek

remarked. "Although I would like to make a study of
the anatomy of creatures from this wor—country. But I
can only do so if I come by them in a natural manner."

"You mean that if I have to shoot something for self
defence or food, it's all right for you to study its body?"
Dusty said.

"The creature is dead then so there is no objection,"
agreed Adek.

"Shall I shoot you something for camp meat if I get
the chance?" asked Dusty.

"No!" snorted Vaza. "I am sorry, Dusty, but I feel
very strongly on that subject. Anyway, we have a sufficient supply of food and do not need more."

"Do you kill many times, Dusty?" asked Jarrel.

"I do some hunting for meat, or to get rid of a stock-
killing bear, cougar or wolf. I don't go hunting just to
hang a set of horns on the wall."

"You have also killed men?"

"Only when I've had to," Dusty answered, feeling no
offence at the words; which puzzled him when he came
to think back on the conversation. "This is a wild
country, rough and growing. There's not much law
here, often all there is comes from what a man can bring
himself."

"Does that not make for tyranny?" asked Adek.

"Sometimes," Dusty admitted. "But mostly the
people themselves end that sort before they get far."

While the wagon rolled on southwards, the travellers
continued their discussion. Dusty did not know whether
he had cleared up any points of his outlook, but found
no change in the party's friendly attitude and even Vaza
seemed to be mollified after her indignation over his
views about animals.

That evening they made camp by a spring on the edge
of wooded land. While the men attended to their work

of horse welfare and wood-gathering, Vaza prepared another of the meals which so intrigued Dusty the previous night. Again she used only the one pan, of that Dusty felt sure from the glances he took as he guided Adek and Jarrel in their work with the horses, yet the meal once more consisted of potatoes, vegetables and meat.

"Will you take a walk with me when we have eaten, Dusty?" said Vaza as he prepared to ask how she managed the culinary feat.

"Why sure, if Adek and Jarrel don't mind," Dusty answered.

"Is there any reason why we should?" smiled Adek.

"Vaza will be safe in your company," Jarrel went on.

"And it would be unwise for her to go alone," Adek continued.

"That's for sure," Dusty admitted.

"You will make me believe that you have no wish to come with me," Vaza remarked gently.

"If that's what I'm doing, I'll stop," grinned Dusty. "We'll go as soon as you're ready."

"Go right away," Adek said. "Jarrel and I will wash the dishes for you."

"You wouldn't want to come along, sir?" asked Dusty.

"You would not wish me to," replied the old man.

"I only asked hoping you'd say no," Dusty answered. "When you're ready, Vaza."

For a moment the girl looked straight at Jarrel, although neither of them spoke. Then she rose and smiled at Dusty. "I'm ready. Let us leave before they change their minds about washing the dishes."

While walking from the camp, the girl looked up at the skies. Overhead a half moon shed feeble light and stars twinkled. Something which Dusty took to be a shooting-star flickered across the sky above them, leaving a trail of red behind in its passage.

"Do you think that there might be people living on other stars and planets, Dusty?" asked the girl.

"I never gave it much thought," he replied. "But I don't see why there shouldn't be."

"What do you think they would look like?"

"Like us, I reckon. Why?"

"I was curious. How would they be received if they came here?"

"Well, first off they'd have to have something better than we've got to get here," Dusty drawled, wondering what sparked off such a train of thought in the girl's head.

"How do you mean?" Vaza asked.

"The only way we can get into the air is by using a balloon and there's only three ways a man can go in one of them. Upwards, whichever the wind's blowing and down. I don't reckon that a man could go high enough to reach even the moon. So happen you're figuring that somebody from up there's going to come down, don't worry none."

"You're laughing at me," Vaza snorted.

"What started all that off anyway?" Dusty inquired.

"I'm a scientist———"

"And a right pretty one at that."

"But I——— Oh, look there, Dusty!"

Following the direction of the girl's pointing finger, Dusty saw a familiar shape waddling ahead of them, headed towards the trees. On hearing the girl's voice, the shape halted and looked back, but showed no inclination to flight.

"A porcupine," Dusty grunted and reached for his left side Colt.

"Yes," agreed the girl and started to move forward.

"Hold it, hot-head!" Dusty warned, catching her arm. "That damned thing's got spikes under its fur. Happen you go too close, you learn just how sharp they can be."

"I know of its defence," Vaza answered. "But I wish it no harm."

"Maybe it wouldn't know *that*," Dusty said dryly, watching the shape waddle on its way. "I've seen what those spines can do to a hunting dog, bear or cougar that went too close. And I'd be showing Adek a mighty good example of how I looked out for you if I take you back with porcupine spines stuck all over you."

"Let me go, please!" she hissed, trying to free herself.

"Not unless you promise not to go too close."

"Dusty," she breathed. "You are concerned about what happens to me."

The anger which had glowed in her eyes died off again with the realisation and she looked straight at him.

"Of course I am," Dusty replied.

Vaza's hand sought for his, taking it and holding it gently. "Come," she said. "And have no fear, I will be safe. To please you, I will take no chances."

Hand in hand, they followed the porcupine, which showed no concern at their presence. Secure in its protection against almost any enemy, the porcupine continued its journey until reaching the foot of an elm tree. Hefting itself erect, it gripped the trunk as high as possible with its forelegs, then pressing down with its flat, powerful tail, it walked upwards with the hind feet until its body almost doubled. Using a repetition of the move, and looking like an enormous caterpillar in motion, the porcupine climbed upwards until lost among the branches.

"This is the first time I have seen a porcupine climb,"

Vaza remarked. "What an amazing animal it is."

"You'll change your mind happen one gets in among your meat," Dusty answered.

"Do your porcupines eat meat then? I always assumed that they, being rodents, lived on vegetable matter."

"One of the Eastern scientists who came visiting allowed that the porky was after the salt we use to cure and preserve stored meat and gnawed the meat to get it."

"That's possible," agreed the girl, then directed another glance into the sky. "Come, let's see if we can find something more among the trees."

They walked on for a time, listening to the night noises and trying to find the creatures which caused them. All the time Dusty kept hold of the girl's hand, feeling it warm and soft in his palm. The scream of an owl as it dropped down on to some fear-paralysed prey caused Vaza to draw involuntarily closer to Dusty. Freeing his hand, he slipped it around the girl's shoulders and held her at his side. For a moment Vaza tried to draw away, then, as if deciding that she liked the security his strong arm gave, remained unstruggling in his grasp.

Failing to locate the owl and it's victim, Dusty and the girl walked on. They came on to a racoon searching under a tree, but it lumbered away with the usual surprising speed of its kind.

"Your animals are much less trusting than the creatures of my country," Vaza commented.

"Most wild critters are," Dusty replied. "Especially after they've been hunted for a spell."

"I suppose that is the reason," the girl said regretfully.

"Don't you hunt in your country?"

"Of course not."

"Not even for food or clothing?"

"We have no need."

"Just what country do you come from, Vaza?"

"You would not know it, Dusty."

Clearly the girl did not want to go further into the matter, so Dusty respected her desire and asked no more questions. Instead, he drew the girl closer to him and felt her arm slip around his waist, move and then return.

"It's a pity that there's not a full moon tonight," Dusty remarked.

"Why?"

"They do say it has an effect on some folks."

"You mean turns a man into a werewolf?" asked Vaza.

"Shucks, no," grinned Dusty. "I mean it's supposed to make a pretty gal feel romantic."

"And then what?"

"Well, happen she was with a feller she liked, she'd let him put his arms around her like this," Dusty drawled, stopping, facing Vaza and slipping his arms about her waist.

"Then what would she do?" asked the girl in a low voice.

"Then she'd maybe let him kiss her."

"What is that?"

"It's one of the customs of the country," Dusty replied and bent his face towards the girl.

At first her lips felt cold and unresponsive. Then her arms tightened around Dusty and she began to kiss him back. On being released, she staggered back a pace and put her hand to her body.

"I—I liked it," she gasped.

"I'd sure hope so," Dusty answered.

"But I am a scientist———"

"You're a real pretty girl, too."

"But I have been trained for my work————"

"Maybe I can offer you a different kind of work," Dusty suggested. "Real permanent work, too."

"It's no use, Dusty," the girl sobbed. "It can never be. Let's go back!"

"If that's what you want," Dusty said quietly.

"It is not—I don't know what I want," moaned the girl. "This feeling I have. It is—I don't know what it is."

"I don't do this with every girl I meet," Dusty told her.

"That I believe," Vaza replied. "You want me, Dusty————"

"To marry me," he answered.

"That cannot be!"

"Why? Because we come from different countries?"

"Not countries, Dusty. Different————"

Vaza chopped off her words, turning and looking in the direction of the camp. Turning, Dusty also looked and although the fire could not be seen for the trees, caught a glimpse of a single brilliant white flash such as had attracted his interest the previous night.

"Different what, Vaza?" he asked gently.

"We have different backgrounds. More so than you can ever understand," she answered. "Please, Dusty, take me back to the camp."

"Sure, Vaza. I'm sorry if I've offended you."

"You have not," the girl cried. "Please, Dusty, take me back."

CHAPTER TWELVE

Tracks of Unshod Horses

During the walk back to the camp, Vaza never spoke a word. She kept away from Dusty and he did not offer to touch her again. At the camp, the two men made no comment on the girl's return apart from asking if she had seen anything of interest.

"The wild life is easily frightened," she replied. "Coming close enough to make a study will not be easy."

"Why do you think the animals are afraid, Dusty?" asked the old man.

"Instinct, I reckon. And up this way they're enough people for the critters to have been hard hunted."

"We hope to make a permanent camp somewhere," Adek commented. "Stay for a good period of time and make an exhaustive study. Where would you suggest?"

"That depends," Dusty replied. "How far are you willing to go to make your camp?"

"I don't understand," Adek said.

"Well, the best place I could think of would be down on the OD Connected ranch, my Uncle Devil's spread. But that's in Rio Hondo country, Texas. You'd be safe there———"

"From what?" Jarrel inquired.

"This's a rough country, like I said. Down there, Vaza can find most of the animals she'll see up here and a few more. Uncle Devil's got a mighty fine library that ought to interest Adek and we'll maybe even find something for you, Jarrel."

"The idea has possibilities," remarked Adek. "No matter where we go, we will attract attention."

"Down home, you'll be free to do as you want," Dusty promised. "And nobody's likely to bother you."

"It is an important decision, Adek," the girl remarked.

"One which cannot be answered immediately or without thought," agreed the old man. "We will think on it for a day or so, then give you our reply, Dusty."

Shortly after, the party retired to their beds. Dawn found them on the move and travelling south at a fair speed. With four powerful horses drawing the wagon, they covered a steady thirty miles a day, seeing no other human beings all that day, although Dusty watched their back-trail. While he did not expect to have further trouble from Gartree, he believed that precautions cost nothing.

They made camp out on the open range that night, ate well and sat about the fire for a time discussing the Civil War. A strange drowsiness came over Dusty and after he went to bed, he knew nothing until Vaza woke him the following morning. A disturbed expression played on her face, worry mingled with delight in a way he found hard to understand.

"You are well, Dusty?" she asked.

"Never felt better," he replied. "Lordy lord, though, I must have slept real heavy last night. I can't remember hearing anybody keep the fire going."

"This surprises you?"

"I reckon to be a light sleeper when I'm on the trail.

It must be all this good food I'm getting."

"Then come and have some more," she smiled. "Also come to listen to Adek's news. I think you will like it."

On rising, Dusty gave a grunt as a momentary dizziness struck him. Almost as if expecting the attack, Vaza shot out a hand, caught his arm and steadied him before he could stagger.

"Whooee!" Dusty exclaimed. "I must have slept a whole heap too hard."

"Yes," agreed the girl. "Are you all right?"

"Sure. The last time I felt that way was after spending four nights without sleep during the War. When I got back to our camp, I hit the hay and slept for twenty-four hours. Felt even worse than just now when I woke."

"It is over now?"

"Will you let go if I say yes?"

"Of course."

"Then I've a good mind to say no."

"I see you have recovered," smiled Vaza and removed her hand.

At the table, Adek and Jarrel directed appraising glances in Dusty's direction, inquired how he slept and, unless he made a mistake, showed relief when he gave them the same answer passed to the girl.

"We have consulted, Dusty," Adek said. "And it has been decided that we may accept your kind offer."

"*Bueno*, sir," Dusty said. "I'll do my best to see that you don't regret it."

"Hello the camp," called a voice from a rim overlooking the camp. "Can I come in?"

"Come right ahead," Dusty answered, looking up at a lone rider who appeared.

Watching the rider approach, Dusty formed certain

conclusions. First the man was a cowhand, not a hired killer. Second, unless Dusty misjudged, the newcomer had followed a cowhand habit recently. Sloughing in his saddle, head drooping and clothing dishevelled, all seemed to indicate the approaching man suffered from the effects of a recent celebration.

"Good morning," Adek greeted as the cowhand dismounted slowly and carefully. "You are just in time for breakfast."

A look of nausea and anguish crossed the cowhand's unshaven face. "No food, thank you most to death. I'd sure admire a cup of coffee though, ma'am."

"Are you ill?" gasped Vaza.

"I'm a dying cowboy, ma'am," said the newcomer. "And I'm scared that I'm going to live and suffer."

"That must have been some whing-ding you had last night, *amigo*," Dusty grinned. "Don't worry, Vaza, he'll be all right with a cup of coffee inside him."

"Spoken like a medical man, friend, or a man who knows what it is to suffer this ways," the cowhand replied. "Which same, you're also a right smart guesser. That sure was a whing-ding last night. Never again though, that's for sure."

"How many times've you said *that*?" asked Dusty.

"This's the first time I've ever meant it," answered the cowhand. "When I start seeing things that aren't there———"

"What sort of things?" asked Adek.

"There you've got me. See, last night I was in at Cassidy's bar in Linton. Ole Cassidy's celebrating having a son and tossing free drinks around. Coming back to home this way, I saw a damned great—asking your pardon, ma'am—I saw this damned great black thing come down out of the sky."

"A bird?" asked Dusty, wondering at the startled

glances his companions exchanged.

"Not unless it was a mighty tough one. Flames shot down from under it as it come down. Man oh man! I don't know where Cassidy gets his free-giving liquor, or what goes into it. But happen it makes a man see things like that, I'm starting to buy my own."

"You did not go closer to this thing?" Jarrel inquired.

"Not me, friend," stated the cowhand. "My old pappy never gave me anything but advice that was mostly wrong. Only wise thing he ever told me was that when a man's likker made him start seeing things, he should lay down and take him a good, long sleep. Which's what I done."

"Then you do not believe you saw anything?" said Adek, sounding relieved.

"I know I didn't," the cowhand answered firmly. "Religious folks like you wouldn't know anything about these things—or maybe you do, way you keep preaching against the evils of strong drink."

"Where did you see that thing?" Dusty drawled.

"You meant where did I didn't see it," corrected the cowhand. "This's one time I wouldn't be pleasured to see something that come from a whisky bottle. Anyways, if I'd seen it, it'd've come down—— Hey, it'd've come down not far from here. Right where— where that burned-out circle up there is."

Following the direction of the cowhand's pointing finger and startled gaze, Dusty saw a large blackened circle burned in the green grass some hundred or so yards from the spot on which they camped.

"That was there yesterday," Jarrel commented, just a shade too quickly, Dusty thought.

"I remember seeing it and meant to ask you what you thought caused it," Adek went on.

"Funny," the cowhand put in. "I've rid this range plenty and I can't remember seeing it."

"Have this cup of coffee," Vaza interrupted, placing it before the young man.

"Thank you kindly, ma'am," answered the cowhand. "I ought to have expected to see things once them lights started flashing."

"How'd you mean, cowboy?" Dusty inquired.

Taking a long sip at the coffee, the young man shuddered. "You know. Real bright white flashes, like when somebody smacks you on the nose unexpected. Saw them in what looked like this direction just before that thing came down—or didn't come down. Ooh! Never again, that's for sure."

"Shall we prepare to move out, Dusty?" asked Adek. "If we are to go to Texas with you, we have a long journey ahead."

"Sure," agreed Dusty.

"I'll be riding soon's I've done this coffee," the cowhand commented. "Don't mention what I told you, friend. I wouldn't want folks to think I can't hold my likker."

"Do you believe he saw anything, Dusty?" asked Jarrel as they hitched the wagon team.

"What could he have seen?" Dusty countered. "Have you ever been drunk?"

"Drunk? No. I can't say I have."

"A man'd have to be real drunk to see things like that."

"But it is possible?"

"I suppose it is," Dusty grunted and went to saddle his paint.

While preparing his horse for travel, Dusty flicked glances at the burned circle and felt sure that it had not been there on the previous night. Yet he could not see how it might have been formed. To burn the green grass in such a manner would take considerable heat and he knew how little fuel they carried.

"Damn it," he growled, tightening the girths. "What else but likker could have caused that jasper to see what he says he saw? If there'd been anything like he said, the horses would be spooked *loco*."

By the time he finished saddling the horse, Dusty found the others ready to roll. Something about the wagon looked different. Only a small thing, but one Dusty noticed. In some way, the wagon seemed to ride lower than on the previous night. It almost seemed that a heavier load rode inside, but that was impossible unless something had been put aboard while he slept. There was nowhere within several miles from the wagon at which fresh supplies could be bought. Dusty tried to tell himself imagination caused the sagging. Certainly the horses did not appear to be putting any more effort in starting the wheels turning as they dug in their calked shoes—calked! Dusty had examined the shoes of the team as part of his nightly ritual. While the shoe Morley put on the paint showed signs of wear, Dusty could see none on the shoes of the team horses.

"Are you ready, Dusty?" called Adek.

"All ready," Dusty replied, watching the cowhand mount. "It must have been the whisky," he told himself. "What in hell else could it have been?"

The party moved on again and Dusty tried to shake off the nagging feeling that something beyond his comprehension happened while he slept the previous night. None of the trio referred to the cowhand's story again and Dusty let the matter drop even if he could not forget it.

For three days the party continued their journey, putting a steady thirty miles behind them during the travelling time. Things went smoothly. At night Dusty remained in the camp and saw no recurrence of the brilliant flashing lights. To all intents and purposes, he might have been travelling with a normal party. Cheerful discussion went on, with Adek showing a remarkable knowledge of many subjects—and just as remarkable an ignorance on others.

Naturally Vaza's reactions interested Dusty most. The girl still rode on the outside of the wagon box, showing interest in everything she saw and bombarding Dusty with her questions. Yet at night she tried to avoid close contact with him. Instinctively Dusty knew that the girl wanted to be close to him, yet some fear held her back. Try as he would, Dusty could not pierce the barrier between them. All she would say, when he tried, was that too many things stood between them for it to ever work.

So matters stood towards evening of the fourth day after their meeting with the cowhand. Having crossed the Oklahoma line, Dusty took them from the trail followed since leaving Bainesville and headed directly across country in the direction of Bent's Ford. Doing so swung them away from the better populated areas of the Indian Nations and, apart from the cowhand, they had seen no sign of human life.

Seeing a fairly wide stream ahead, Dusty told the others that he would ride ahead and ensure that they could cross at the points towards which they headed. As Dusty rode closer, he saw that the place ahead offered a convenient crossing, the banks sloping down to an area of firm gravel that appeared to continue clear across and up the other side. Further proof of the possibility of an easy ford showed in the multitude of animal tracks left in the gravel.

While Dusty had not the Ysabel Kid's skill as a

tracker, he knew something of reading sign. Looking like a long-nailed oil man's hand print, a coon's feet left their marks on the edge of the stream before disappearing into the water. The dog-like pads of a wolf mingled with the dainty, sharp-pointed liver-shaped hooves of white-tailed deer.

All that and more he saw, but ignored the signs of passing wild life. His main interest directed itself on some marks made after the rest of the sign, comparatively recently or Dusty missed his guess. Roughly oval marks with a heart-shaped piece forcing in at the rear. That particular type of track had no duplicate. One might mistake deer and elk tracks, confuse the line left by a dog with that of a wolf—but there was no mistaking the marks caused by a horse's hooves.

Merely finding horses' hoof prints would have caused Dusty no concern, but the four sets before him told a significant story. One point of identification normally set aside and showed the horse's tracks plainly. The shoe left an unmistakable addition to the rest of the mark—only the tracks before Dusty lacked that addition.

Numbers of wild horses roamed the plains country and never felt the touch of an iron shoe; but not in the Indian Nations. Every wild horse had long since been captured by the Indians living on the reservations. The Indian never shod his horse, never gave its feet any protection.

Dusty knew that the riders who crossed the stream earlier that day had been riding unshod horses. Which meant they were most likely Indians.

CHAPTER THIRTEEN

Vaza's Change of Mind

The discovery of the tracks did not worry Dusty unduly
and he saw no need to disturb his companions by mentioning his find. For the most part the Indians in the
Oklahoma reservations, watched over by fair-sized
garrisons of the U.S. Army, prevented as far as possible
from owning firearms and other weapons, dependent on
the white man for food and shelter, tended to keep the
peace. Of course a small party of whites might be killed
and their property looted if such could be done with
small risk or chance of detection; but Dusty doubted if
four Indians would chance making mischief against so
nearly equal odds.

Despite his thoughts, Dusty could not shake off an
uneasy feeling that they were being watched as they
crossed the river and made camp. Try as he might, he
could see nothing of the watchers in the tree-dotted,
broken, rolling land around him, so he helped set up the
camp.

Night came without any sight or hint of hostile pres-
ences. After a meal and the usual discussion, the travellers prepared to go to sleep. Dusty had mentioned
his uneasiness when, showing that remarkable facility
for guessing his thoughts, Vaza asked what made him so

nervous. However, he told the others that there was little to fear, and believed it himself. He did insist that they brought the horses in and fastened them with rope to the side of the wagon instead of allowing them to graze hobbled as on other nights.

Settling down in his blankets, Dusty kept one of his Colts in his hand. He could hear the coyotes yipping all around the camp and counted it as a good sign. Soon he drifted off to sleep and silence fell on the camp.

Shortly after midnight, a squirrel chattered its warning in the trees down by the river. All around the camp, the coyotes continued their nightly serenade although there had been a slight period of silence to the west shortly before the squirrel gave tongue.

Crouching beyond the light of the fire, Walks Quiet, son of a one-time Kaddo war chief, studied the sleeping camp. Knife in hand, he moved forward in the silent way which gave him his name. Two of his companions edged out a short distance behind, making for the wagon in accordance to the plan made earlier. Out in the night, the fourth member of the band crouched on his haunches and gave life-like coyote yips to prevent any chance of the white-eye victim noticing the silence of the animals in that direction, a method advocated by the battle-tried veterans who told tales around the reservation fires of the glories of the war-trail.

The quartet were young bucks who reached manhood too late to ride to war, but the spirit of their war-loving ancestors flowed through them. In the old days they would have ridden on raiding parties, gaining praise and the adoration of the tribe's maidens when they returned with coups counted and trophies to show. Such things could still be done, although not on the grand old scale. A small party of whites might be found and accorded the time-honored treatment. Of course, one could not return flourishing scalps and leading horses loaded with loot that might be traced back should the victims' bodies be found. However, Burkee, the trader, took such things and gave attractive, praise-winning goods in return, without ever questioning the bringer's right to possession.

On seeing the wagon cross the stream, Walks Quiet and his companions held a debate on their actions. Odds of three to four did not strike them as being good medicine, until they gave thought to the three men they would attack. Having an extensive knowledge of white men, Walks Quiet figured two of the three would give them no trouble. They wore the clothing of the white-eye god-men; such were neither fighting men nor went armed. Which left the third male member of the party. No meek, defenceless god-man, that one, but a ride-plenty, a cowhand such as rode herd on the white-eyes' spotted buffalo herds that came through the Indian Nations. Every ride-plenty knew how to fight with the guns he wore.

So, Walks Quiet decided, the ride-plenty must die first, before he could wake and use his guns. Then the others would be easy. Kill the men and the girl—but she must not die too soon or before he and his companions took their pleasure.

Stepping on silent feet, Walks Quiet drew closer to the sleeping Texan. From the steady rise and fall of the blankets, the Indian knew his victim slept deeply and without any suspicion of danger.

"Dusty!" Jarrel's voice roared in the small Texan's head. "Wake up!"

Instantly Dusty woke to see and understand the meaning of the shape looming above him. A life-time spent in dangerous situations had taught Dusty to come straight from sleep to wakefulness without any tran-

sitory period of dull-witted lack of comprehension.
Seeing the Indian, he knew all that was necessary to
send his lightning fast reactions into operation.

An expression of amazement came to Walks Quiet's
face as he saw what should have been a helpless victim
suddenly, and without any reason that the Indian could
see or hear, change into a deadly menace to his very life.
His advance had been made with silence which brought
him his man's name and he knew that the Texan slept
deeply, undisturbed by anything Walks Quiet did. Even
as Walks Quiet tried to understand, flame lashed from
the barrel of Dusty's Army Colt and a .44 bullet drove
up under the Indian's chin to burst out of the top of his
head.

Rolling from his blankets, even as Walks Quiet
toppled over backwards, Dusty turned his attention to
the other two Indians. At the shot, they halted in their
tracks, flung a startled glance towards where their
leader dropped dead and saw the proposed victim turn
to face them. Knowing that their Green River knives
were no match for a revolver in capable hands, the
braves whirled on their heels and bounded swiftly into
the darkness.

"Thanks, Jarrel," Dusty said, rising and looking to
where the two men emerged from beneath the wagon.
"You yelled just in time."

"They came to kill us," Adek gasped in a disbelieving
voice. "And to do far worse to Vaza. But why? We have
done them no harm."

"It's the Indian way," Dusty replied, holstering his
Colt and then buckling on his belt. He picked up the
carbine and went on, "I'd best scout around and make
sure they've gone. Keep Vaza in the wagon until after
we've moved the body."

"Be careful, Dusty," the girl called.

"I'll do that, but you stay inside that wagon."

With that Dusty left the clearing. The delicate and dangerous business of scouting against hostile Indians held his full attention and prevented him from wondering how Adek guessed so accurately at the attackers' intentions.

After Dusty left, the girl swung down from the wagon. She gave a shudder as she looked towards Walks Quiet's body, then turned to the men.

"I was too frightened to move when I realised what they meant to do," she said. "Thank you, Jarrel."

"That's the first time I have ever been able to communicate with Dusty," the man answered. "I can understand him sometimes, but until tonight never reached him. It is fortunate that I did, for I forgot to shout."

"It happened in the town when the young man meant to kill Dusty," Vaza said. "I reached him then. Sometimes I think I can almost get through, especially when we are close. Perhaps the stimulus of impending danger makes him more receptive."

"That's possible," admitted Adek. "You have a great liking for that young man, Vaza."

"I have. If only there was some way we could find out———"

"The records of the Salem party were destroyed, so we do not know if these people are the same organically as we are," Adek remarked. "But we have the means to find out."

"You mean that body there?" the girl breathed.

"It conforms with the requirements," Adek answered. "But we must move swiftly before our young friend returns. I don't think that it would be wise to let him know what we do."

"That was the reason for our people's arrest at

Salem,'' Jarrel put in. ''The citizens of the town saw an experiment being carried out. We must take no chances this time. True I have a weapon, but I have no wish to use it.''

If there had been a witness to the scene, he would have sworn that the group stood in silence, for their lips never moved and no word came audibly. Turning, the two men went to where the body lay and lifted it from the ground to carry it and place it inside the wagon. Then Jarrel went to make up the fire, but Adek and the girl remained inside.

Dusty spent a good hour or more searching the woods. While he heard the sound of hooves departing, he could not say for sure how many horses left and knew enough about Indians not to accept that each horse carried a rider. Making a thorough scout led him at last to believe that the remaining trio of raiders had gone, instead of one taking the horses off out of hearing and leaving his companions to make a second attempt at stealing horses or grabbing sóme other loot once the camp settled down again. When satisfied, Dusty made his way back through the trees and towards the fire's glow.

''Is all well, Dusty?'' asked Jarrel when the small Texan walked back.

''They've gone and I don't reckon they'll be back,'' Dusty replied. ''Where's Adek and Vaza?''

''In the wagon.''

''Is Vaza———?''

''She is a little shaken by the experience, but nothing more.'' Jarrel replied and followed the direction of the other's gaze. ''We thought it advisable to remove the body and so carried it off into the trees.''

''Good thinking,'' Dusty drawled. ''You're sure that Vaza's all right?''

Before Jarrel could answer, any doubts Dusty might

have felt received an answer. The girl sprang from the
wagon, her face alight with such happiness that Dusty
wondered what caused it. Rushing forward, she threw
her arms around his neck and clung to him.

"Dusty!" she gasped. "It's all right. We are the
same."

"Hey, easy there now," he replied, gently freeing
himself. "What do you mean by 'We're the same'?"

"I—I meant, I was pleased to see you safe," she
replied, her eyes glowing with a warmth that stirred
Dusty more than he could imagine.

"I'm safe," he agreed. "But you———"

"Let us walk together for a time and I will explain,"
the girl said.

"If that's what you want," Dusty drawled gently.

"It is. And it will help me recover. I will not sleep
unless I can forget the happenings of tonight."

"I wouldn't want you to lie awake all night," Dusty
smiled. "Let's go."

Hand in hand, he and the girl left the fire. In passing
his bed, Dusty laid down the carbine. Then, slipping his
arm around the girl's waist, he walked off into the
darkness.

"We are the same, Dusty," she breathed as they entered the wooded land, "and there is nothing to prevent
us———"

"Yes, Vaza?"

"You asked me to stay with you. Do you wish it
still?"

"You know I do," Dusty stated.

"Even though you know so little about me, where I
am come from, what I am."

"I know all I want to know."

"Then I accept."

With that she turned to face him and her mouth

reached for his in a long, passionate kiss.

"We'll leave getting the engagement ring until we get home," Dusty told the girl as they separated.

"What is that?" she asked.

"One of the customs of the country," he said with a smile and explained.

"In my country, we signify it in a different manner," she said.

"What is it?" asked Dusty.

"This," she replied, and drew him down to the ground.

Time passed and the girl nestled warmly in Dusty's arms. "What do you think of my country's customs?" she whispered.

"We have it over here," Dusty admitted. "But that doesn't stop me liking it."

Much to Dusty's surprise, on returning with Vaza at dawn, Adek and Jarrel showed no disapproval or objections to their being away all night.

"Congratulations, Dusty," Jarrel said when the Texan announced his intention to marry the girl. "You will be a good husband for her."

"I hope that everything is as you wish," Adek went on. "It is not the first time one of us has settled in a country during an expedition, but not always with success."

"This time it will be," Dusty promised.

"I think it will," smiled the old man. "My best wishes, children. Now, come and eat."

"We'll have to call at the sheriff's office in Linton," Dusty remarked as they sat eating a breakfast almost as good as Vaza would have cooked. "I'll tell him about last night and he'll warn the reservation agent. Maybe I'd best take a look at the buck I shot so's I can describe him."

"We—We buried the body after you left us last night, Dusty," Adek said hurriedly. "Is that not the custom of your land?"

"Sure, although most folks wouldn't do it for an Indian," Dusty answered. "Maybe I'd best take a look just the same."

"We removed the clothing and trinkets from the body," Jarrel put in. "Will they do for identification?"

"I reckon they will," agreed Dusty. "And I wasn't too eager to start digging the body up at that."

After eating, the party moved out from their camping ground. As usual Vaza rode so that she could talk to Dusty; but showed no interest in anything but the small Texan.

"It will not be easy to fit into your world," she warned. "There is so much I must learn. Cooking——"

"You cook real good," Dusty objected.

"Cook!" the girl laughed. "All the food we eat was prepared before we left and only requires heating in water to be ready."

"You mean that it comes out of a can?" asked Dusty.

"In a manner of speaking," she agreed. "Do you have such food?"

"Air-tights? Sure we have them, but nothing like you can turn out. Corn, tomatoes, peaches, milk's about all we can. You look like you've got everything."

"Practically everything," smiled the girl. "So you see, you are not marrying a good cook."

"We can live on corn, tomatoes, peaches and milk if we have to," Dusty grinned back. "Or maybe have Adek send us boxes of your stuff over after he goes home."

"I think it will be better if I learn to cook your way," said the girl seriously. "Unfortunately I was trained as a scientist and did not learn such things."

"I'll just have to live with it," Dusty drawled. "There's Linton in the distance."

Despite his interest in the radiant-faced girl at his side, Dusty studied a trio of cowhands who approached from the other end of the town. He read trouble in their manner of coming. Instead of the usual rowdy rush, the trio rode slowly, the outer men supporting the one in the center as he sat doubled over, face ashy and pain-lined, wet with sweat, hands clutching at the saddlehorn.

"Where at's the doctor, friend?" called the man at the right to a passing town dweller.

"Out of town," came the reply. "He's———"

Before the man could continue, the central cowhand let out a moan and slumped forward weakly, hung for a moment and then started to slip out of his saddle. Jumping the paint forward, Dusty left its back and ran forward. So swiftly did he move, that he reached and caught the slipping man, holding him from the ground.

"Back those horses off!" Dusty barked. "Move it, damn you!"

His voice brought action from the two young men. Recognising the tone, they obeyed without question. One grabbed their companion's mount and together they walked their horses back and allowed Dusty to lower the groaning figure to the ground.

Showing a remarkable agility for so old a man, Adek sprang from the wagon and darted forward. He dropped to his knees alongside the cowhand, reaching out to draw aside and up the shirt, exposing the lower stomach.

"How long has he been like this?" Adek asked, looking to where the other two cowhands dismounted.

"Started complaining of pains in his belly around breakfast, but we thought it was nothing more'n an attack of the grippe. Then when he got worse, our trail boss told us to bring him into Linton to see the doctor.''

"Then he's come for nothing," the townsman put in. "Doc left town for the Neal place last night."

"Can he be fetched back?" Adek inquired.

"It's half a day's ride up to the north," the man replied.

"There is not that much time to spare," gritted the old man, looking down.

"Can you do anything to help, Adek?" Dusty said.

"I could—but———"

"Mister," one of the cowhands interjected. "Joey here's a good pard. Happen you can help him; well, we haven't any money, but the boss'll let us draw on our end-of-drive pay."

"The money doesn't come into it," Adek snapped. "I can do all that is needed provided———"

"Do it, Adek!" Vaza said. "Please do it."

"Remember, Adek," warned Jarrel. "It was performing such an operation that first aroused suspicions in Salem."

"Hell, fire, Jarrel!" Dusty growled. "We've advanced some since then. It's almost two hundred years back that happened. Go ahead, if you reckon you can help him, Adek. I've seen men taken that way before and both times they died."

"Can you do it, mister?" asked the second cowhand.

"Of course. An appendectomy is a simple operation and I have all I need in the wagon."

"Doc's office is right along the street, mister," the townsman said. "His missus'll let you use it."

"Then we will take him there after I have put him under sedation," Adek declared.

"How's that, mister?" asked one of the cowhands.

"Make him sleep," snapped the old man. "Vaza,

bring me all we will need. You must assist me.''

"Of course," the girl agreed and disappeared into the wagon.

"How'd you plan to put him to sleep?" Dusty inquired.

"With a—drug," replied Adek.

"He can't drink it," Dusty pointed out.

"Nor will need to, although it is soluble in liquid and can be used that way. Have no fear, Dusty, I know what I am doing."

"If I doubted that, I'd stop you," Dusty informed the old man.

Carrying a small box and a bottle, Vaza left the wagon and hurried to Adek's side. She knelt alongside the groaning, writhing cowhand, removed the cap from the bottle and poured a small quantity of the powder through his open lips. After a few seconds, the moaning died off and writhing ended, until the cowhand lay still and apparently in a deep sleep.

"Now you can move him in safety," Adek told the waiting men. "He will sleep long enough, and feel nothing, for me to do my work."

"That's mighty potent stuff," Dusty remarked. "Does it take much to make a man sleep?"

"Varying amounts," the girl answered, stoppering the bottle. "It all depends upon the length of time one wishes the receiver to sleep."

Watching the two cowhands and a couple of townsmen raise the still form, a thought struck Dusty. Given a dose of that stuff, a man would sleep through any disturbance—even brightly flashing lights close by his bed.

CHAPTER FOURTEEN

The Peaceful Valley

After listening to Dusty's story, the sheriff dropped his eyes to the bundle of clothing, cheap trinkets and knife on his desk, then raised them again to study the small Texan.

"I'll pass them on to the reservation agent as soon as I can."

"Is that all you intend to do?" Jarrel, standing at Dusty's side, asked.

"Just what had you in mind for me to do?" inquired the lawman, turning his gaze from Dusty to Jarrel.

"There were at least two more Indians present. Do you not intend to make an effort to find them before they attack some other travellers?"

"You tell me what to do, and dog-my-cats if I don't go on out and try it," growled the sheriff. "What's the first move, mister?"

"You could try to locate the two by learning who owned this clothing and the trinkets we brought to you."

"Sure I could, never would have thought of it all on my own and without help though," said the sheriff, his voice as tired as his face and general appearance. "Thing being, where'd I find out from?"

"Among the Indians on the reservation," Jarrel suggested.

"Mister," the sheriff said patiently. "I don't know what kind of Injuns you're used to, but the kind around here just don't talk to a white lawman. Happen you hadn't buried that one Cap'n Fog shot, we might have found somebody who knew him and could say which of his pards rode with him last night. Even then proving it might not be easy. Could you recognise either of 'em again?"

"I could not," admitted Jarrel. "Perhaps Dusty could."

"Not to swear to in court," Dusty said.

"Then there is nothing you can do, Sheriff?"

"Like I said, tell me what and I'll have a go at doing it. I don't want any young buck thinking he can use my county for his war trials. And don't say send a posse out. I just don't have the men to spare right now. I've just come in and all my deputies are out hunting for four prisoners that broke from a wagon taking them over for trial by Judge Parker at Fort Smith."

"Anybody special, Sheriff?" asked Dusty.

"Special and choice," the lawman replied. "Least some of them. Vic Tetley's the choicest, only he took a bullet during the escape. Then there's a half-breed called Javelina that the Rangers run out of Texas. Which same, Cap'n, happen you know any Rangers, ask 'em to run any more they don't want down south, we've enough of our own. The other two aren't so choice, Buck-Eye Baise and Tom Moon."

"I've heard tell of Javelina," Dusty drawled. "The others don't mean much to me though."

"Tetley's real smart, especially at opening locks. Fact being he opened an Army paymaster's safe and got away with maybe ten thousand dollars that wasn't recovered. Could be that's why the others helped him off after he took lead. Moon and Baise don't run to brains, most likely the other two only took them along to keep them quiet.''

"Which way have they gone?" Dusty asked.

"The Lord knows, and he's not giving any sign. We hadn't trailed them but two miles when we lost their tracks.''

"That figures. Javelina's smarter than a tree full of hoot-owls when it comes to hiding sign. Was it a planned escape do you reckon?''

"If it was, they planned bad,'' the sheriff grunted. "They'd've had horses close to hand, which they hadn't. They was still afoot when we lost them.''

"That's bad,'' Dusty breathed.

"Real bad,'' agreed the sheriff. "And that's why I can't take time to go out hunting a pair of bucks who'll be back on the reservation by now, where I can't touch 'em even if I knew 'em.''

"I don't follow you,'' Jarrel put in.

"It's like I explained one night,'' Dusty told him. "An Indian reservation's Government land and comes under Federal law. A county sheriff has no jurisdiction on it.''

"You explained it,'' Jarrel agreed. "I still do not fully understand your complicated legal system.''

"Don't let that worry you, friend,'' said the sheriff. "Even the folks who made it don't understand it.''

"Let's go, Jarrel,'' Dusty remarked. "Thanks for the time, Sheriff.''

"Sure, Cap'n Fog,'' the sheriff answered and held his hand towards Jarrel. "I'm sorry I jumped you, friend, only I'm a mite tuckered out. I only came in here to put up my shotgun before going home for some sleep then taking off out after Tetley's bunch again.''

"I understand, Sheriff," Jarrel replied, shaking hands then turning to follow Dusty from the office.

"I don't like it, Jarrel, and that's for sure," Dusty said as they returned to the wagon. "Those escaped prisoners want food, a change of clothing, horses and guns. Unless they've got some hid away, they're going to have to steal some."

"There is danger to us?"

"Not as long as we keep our eyes open. I reckon that they'll head for the nearest Indian reservation and hide up, or look for some outlaw hang-out."

"They could not travel far with a wounded man," Jarrel pointed out.

"That's something that puzzles me," Dusty drawled. "I can't see men on the run from trial by 'Hanging' Parker trailing a wounded man along, yet they did."

"Loyalty perhaps?" Jarrel suggested.

"Not where Javelina's concerned. Anyways, we'll just take turns at standing guard every night until we're well clear. Three more days should see us at Bent's Ford and after that we'll have no need to worry."

"No. With your friend on hand there will be no danger."

"Not from a bunch that small," grinned Dusty and wondered what his two all but inseparable *amigos* would say when they heard he planned to marry and settle down. "I wonder how Adek's getting on?"

Almost as the words left Dusty's mouth, a wild cowhand yell rang out along the street, followed by a couple of shots. Jarrel swung around, his face coming as close as Dusty could remember ever seeing it to showing emotion. Down the street a small knot of people crowded towards the front of a house. Judging by the shingle hanging outside the building, Dusty judged it to be the doctor's house. To confirm the idea, he saw Adek and Vaza emerge to be surrounded.

"We must help them!" Jarrel growled.

"Yahoo!" whooped a voice and another shot rang out, its cloud of powder-smoke going into the air. "Ole Joey's going to be all right."

"They don't need help," Dusty drawled. "Cowhands tend to cut loose good and noisy when they're happy."

Certainly the crowd showed no hostility as they accompanied Adek and Vaza towards the wagon. While Linton's citizens often found themselves at odds with celebrating cowhands, the nearness of death made past differences forgotten and all present joined the two young men in the excited delight that the sick man would live.

"The doc here fixed ole Joey up good, friend," the cowhand announced and turned to Adek. "Doc, would it be agin your ways to take a drink?"

"I'm afraid it would," smiled Adek.

Normally such a refusal might have been met with derision if nothing worse, but none of the crowd thought anything wrong in Adek's abstemious habits.

"Well, we're just going to have one to you," grinned the second cowhand. "Yes, sir, Doc. And happen you go out to the herd, the boss'll see to anything you want. We've not got much mon——"

"I want nothing, young man," Adek interrupted. "Now we must be on our way."

"But we wanted to thank you properly," objected the first young man.

"Knowing your friend will live is all the thanks I need," Adek said and Dusty formed the impression that the old man wanted to get away in a hurry. "I have left instructions for his future treatment. He will be well, but unable to ride for some time."

"We'll pick him up on the way south," the cowhand answered. "Come on, gents, let's go and drink to a real good doctor."

Throwing more praise in Adek's direction, the cowhands led the townsmen off in the direction of the saloon. After watching the men go, Adek turned to Dusty and suggested that they left immediately if possible.

"There's nothing to stop us," Dusty replied. "But why the rush, Adek?"

"You know what I have done?" asked the old man.

"Saved a man's life," Dusty replied. "I've seen two men hit by the same illness that cowhand had, and both died. There was a doctor on hand for one of them and he couldn't save the man."

"But it was only appendicitis," Vaza objected.

"That might be an 'only' back at your home, honey," Dusty told her. "But out here it's a killer." Then a thought struck him, although he tried to fight it down.

"I am competent to operate for such a thing and, as long as my instructions are followed, the young man will make a recovery," Adek remarked, answering Dusty's unspoken doubts.

"Then why do you want to leave so fast?" asked Dusty bluntly.

"I act for the best, my friend," Adek replied. "When the doctor returns, he will see and realise what I have done and wish to ask questions. Even if he does not, other people will hear of the cure and come expecting to receive treatment. That was what happened in Salem."

"How do you mean?"

"The party Vaza told you about. One was a doctor and the cures he effected seemed miraculous to the people of the town, for they were far beyond the primitive medical knowledge of the time. So some claimed it to be witchcraft and three of the party died.''

"That won't happen today," Dusty growled.

"Have your people advanced so far, Dusty?" countered Adek. "This is a violent land———"

"But we've grown past believing in witches and magic spells," Dusty replied.

"Probably," smiled the old man. "But take the word of one who has some small experience in these things. If we stay here until the doctor returns, there will be questions asked and the answers may not prove satisfactory. I have done as much as I dared for that young man. More and—well, let us say your people might have thought I performed a miracle. Trust me, Dusty. Believe me when I say that the young man will live. Now let us go, for to stay will bring only complications and possible disaster."

"Please do as Adek says, Dusty," Vaza put in, her eyes on the small Texan's face. "Please, for me."

If anything could have persuaded Dusty, it was the girl's request. He reached out and laid a gentle hand on the old man's shoulder. "I believe you, Adek, and apologise for doubting you. Besides, the sooner we leave, the quicker we reach Texas—and that can't come soon enough for me."

With that, Dusty helped the girl into the wagon and watched the men climb aboard. Mounting his paint, he rode alongside his friends and watched by a few people of the town, the party headed south.

In view of Adek's concern, Dusty raised no objections to the pace Jarrel set once clear of the town. While riding, Dusty turned over in his head the events of the morning and found himself, as he so often had during the journey, more puzzled at the end than before he started. Every instinct he possessed told him that Adek would never have offered to help unless sure that he could do nothing but good. Yet the old man claimed to be a historian, not a doctor. While not knowing what appendicitis might be, Dusty guessed that Adek had performed an operation that might have tried the ability of many a prominent Eastern surgeon.

During the War Dusty had seen many wounded men and listened to Army surgeons discuss the difficulty of operating upon the interior of the body. One of the major difficulties of such an operation was rendering the patient sufficiently unconscious so as to ensure that pain did not drive through and bring about any premature return to consciousness. Chloroform, as developed in the United States in 1831 by Samuel Guthrie, was dangerous in that judging the correct amount could not be done accurately and an over-dose proved fatal. Nitrous Oxide, laughing gas, was just as uncertain in effect. To Dusty's knowledge, no drug known to America's medical science could have equalled the way the powder used by Adek worked.

Once again Dusty found the old question pounding at him. Who were his three companions? From what country did they come? Why had not word leaked out of their remarkable scientific developments? He could find no answer and promised himself that he would force the issue, throw aside his objections to prying into other people's affairs and satisfy his curiosity at the earliest opportunity.

The opportunity did not come for some time. Pushing their horses hard, the party covered almost fifteen miles during the afternoon and might have made more. They had left the trail and travelled across country once more, relying on Dusty's sense of direction to point them towards Bent's Ford. Topping a slope, Jarrel drew rein to let his team catch their breath, and the party looked down into a valley.

"It's beautiful!" Vaza breathed, looking down the wooded slopes to the flower-dotted bottom of the valley, then following the crystal-clear stream which ran through to disappear in bushes heavy with cranberries. "We must stay here for the night. Can we, please?"

"I'm with you, honey," Dusty drawled. "But I'm more interested in that buffalo-grass down there than how the place looks. The horses need a chance to graze well after a haul like we made today. I reckon we've put enough distance between us and Linton, Adek."

"Very well," the old man replied. "Here is where we camp for the night."

While the man cared for the horses, with Dusty showing the other two those extra details necessary with a hard-pushed, lathered team, Vaza slipped away and disappeared into the bushes. At first Dusty thought nothing of the girl's departure, then after she had been away far longer than necessary for what he imagined took her out of sight, he became concerned.

"Vaza!" he shouted. "Where are you?"

"Here," came the girl's voice. "Come and see what I have found."

"Go," smiled Adek tolerantly. "You have shown Jarrel and I all we need to know and we can manage now."

"We can," agreed Jarrel. "But do not stay away too long, I dislike cooking."

"We dislike you having to cook," Adek commented; the first time Dusty had heard anything approaching humor from the old man.

"It could be worse," Dusty warned. "You might have *me* cooking for you."

With that he headed for the bushes and looked

around for the girl. Not until Vaza called again did
Dusty locate her and when he came into sight of the girl,
he could hardly believe his eyes.

Vaza stood by a bush looking in his direction and
smiling. Cradled in her arms, she held an almost full-
grown racoon and, to Dusty's surprise it seemed to
accept the treatment. Not until the coon saw Dusty
approaching did it show any signs of alarm. Even then it
only struggled gently in Vaza's grasp.

"Drop it before it bites you?" Dusty snapped,
knowing just how hard a coon that size could use its
teeth.

"Why should it bite me?" Vaza replied, looking
down at the masked face of the coon. "I mean it no
harm."

With that she set the animal down on the ground and
it waddled away leisurely in the direction of the stream.
Vaza advanced to meet Dusty, her eyes sparkling in the
way he had come to love.

"I came on the coon just before it found a bird's
nest," she said. "The eggs are just about to hatch
and I couldn't let him eat them, although I suppose as a
trained scientist I should not have interfered. In fact
until I met you, I would not have thought of interference in such a basic matter. Look."

Smiling tolerantly, Dusty followed the direction the
girl pointed and saw a catbird's nest among the foliage
of a bush. The birds fluttered in the background,
making the mewing sound which gave them their name.

"Looks just like any other catbird's nest," he said,
noticing the four eggs inside, but seeing nothing to tell
him how near to hatching they might be.

"And to me," Vaza answered. "But the eggs are
ready to hatch. I will watch them when they do. But
now let us go, for you disturb the parent birds."

Taking Dusty's hand in hers, Vaza led him away from the nest and along the path down which the coon disappeared. Before they had gone far, the black and white shape appeared before them. Although the coon looked back, it made no attempt to either run or go into a tree. After standing staring at the girl, who drew slightly ahead of Dusty, the coon continued on its way, acting as if there was not a human being within miles.

Side by side, Vaza and Dusty followed the coon as it ambled along. Up until that day Dusty's sole interest in coons stemmed from their providing good sport and a fine inducement to make hounds sing out trail music. Following the animal, he learned a number of things of interest and answered a few questions that had puzzled him when hunting.

Suddenly Dusty realised that they had been away from the others for over an hour, although circling the open area of the valley in which they made camp.

"We'd best get back to Jarrel and Adek," he told the girl.

"But I wish to make a more extensive study of the raccoon's habits," Vaza objected.

"We've coon down in the Rio Hondo," Dusty replied. "And I don't like being away from the camp for too long. Jarrel's not used to handling the carbine yet."

"You fear that the escaped prisoners may be close?"

"I'd as soon not take a chance. If they're around, the smoke from our campfire might bring them. They're mean and desperate."

"Jarrel is not entirely defenceless," Vaza smiled.

"Maybe not, but I'd as soon not take chances," Dusty answered.

Turning, he and the girl started to walk back in the direction of the camp. The bushes, though thick, were laced with animal tracks and Dusty stuck to one which headed in the right direction. While crossing a place where two paths met, Dusty caught a movement along the other track and swung to obtain a better view. What he saw sent a chill of apprehension ripping through him and caused him to send his left hand across to the butt of the right side Colt. Even as he made the move, he knew it to be no more than a gesture of desperation. An Army Colt did not have sufficient power to deal with the deadly danger which threatened the girl he loved.

Becoming aware of Dusty and Vaza's presence, the bear approaching along the other path halted in its tracks and growled low in its throat. Standing almost four foot high at the shoulder's distinctive hump, the bear had a huge head with a broad muzzle and forehead strongly elevated above the line of the face to give a somewhat concave profile, and smallish, rounded ears placed well apart and far back on the skull. The white tips of the dark brown hair gave the coat a grizzled effect which was terribly significant.

Even without needing to see the great, long claws on the feet, or the wicked canine teeth and broad-crowned crushing molars, Dusty knew what kind of bear stood before him. That was no black bear; to which the old-time Indians apologised before killing with a club and regarded as unworthy of death by arrow or war lance. The bear facing Dusty belonged to the species *Ursus Horribilis Horribilis* and any man who tried to club a Great Plains Grizzly would barely live long enough to regret his folly. Fact being, any man who went up against a grizzly armed with less than the heaviest calibred buffalo rifle asked for trouble in plenty. Certainly an Army Colt—fine man-stopper though it might be—was no weapon with which to face the charge of a grizzly bear.

"Make a run for it, honey," he ordered.

With luck he could hold the bear's attention while the girl made good her escape, but it would cost him his life. Willing, Dusty prepared to make the sacrifice, but Vaza ignored his words. Dusty threw a glance at the girl when she did not move, expecting to find her rigid with terror. No fear showed on Vaza's face, but her eyes glowed luminously as she stared at the bear.

"Have no fear, Dusty," she said and took a step forward. "Do not move whatever you do."

Cold sweat trickled down Dusty's face and he stood like a statue. He noticed that the bear's left ear had been torn in the past by a rifle bullet—an old wound long since healed, which might be termed a small consolation. Such an injury would not make the bear any better disposed towards members of the hated species which gave it.

"Move aside, Vaza," he gritted. "When I shoot, run."

"Dusty!" the girl's voice came back urgently. "Take your hand off your gun."

Why he obeyed, Dusty could not think, but he let the Colt slide back into leather and moved his hand. Then he stood without movement, watching the girl face the bear. Still as stone, the girl continued to stare at the bear and slowly the savage snarling died away. After what seemed like several hours to Dusty, but was only a matter of a minute at most, the bear swung around and began to eat the ripe berries from a near-by bush.

"Let's get the hell out of here," Dusty whispered.

"Very well," the girl replied and turned unconcernedly to walk back to his side. "I hope that I have another opportunity to study a bear."

"I don't!" stated Dusty firmly. "Honey, I was a

tolerable young man until I met you, and want to stay that way for a few years yet.''

"You make a joke?" Vaza asked.

"Only to stop me running away," Dusty replied. "If I hadn't seen it, I'd never believe it was possible. How did you do it?"

"I told you I am a naturalist," Vaza answered. "It is something we are selected for and trained to do. How else could I do my work if I cannot gain the confidence of the animals so that they act naturally in my presence."

"Honey, that bear *didn't* behave naturally—thank God!"

"I don't wish to hurt you, Dusty," Vaza said gently. "But I could have reached the bear far easier if I had been left alone. Your presence disturbed it."

A harsh bark of laughter burst from Dusty before he could stop it. "Well I'll tell you, honey," he said. "That makes us evens. That old bear disturbed me a mite too." He caught the girl and kissed her hard. "Now let's get back to the camp."

CHAPTER FIFTEEN

The End of a Peaceful Day

After the meeting with the grizzly, Dusty escorted Vaza back to the camp. They found that Adek and Jarrel had prepared a meal and during it Dusty told of the incident, but found that his news did not surprise the men. Although he felt decidedly uneasy about having a grizzly prowling so close to the camp—for the big bear showed a partiality to horse-meat—Dusty soon found he did not need to worry.

An explosive snort from his paint brought him spinning around. The bear stood at the edge of the clearing and the paint showed considerable objections to its presence. Even as Dusty threw a glance to his carbine, which leaned against the side of the wagon, Vaza left her seat and walked towards the horse. Dusty no longer felt any concern over the girl approaching his horse, for the paint accepted her and made no attempt to attack her. After a short time the stallion settled down, ignoring the bear which munched a few berries and then ambled on its way once more.

"I'll never know how you do it, honey," Dusty told the girl, "but it sure licks the be-jeesus out of anything I ever saw before. I've seen animal trainers in travelling shows who couldn't do half of what you do."

"I don't understand," Vaza answered.

"That paint of mine knows enough about bears to run a mile to avoid one. But he just stood there and let a damned great silvertip walk by not fifty yards from him. How'd you do it?"

"I have done nothing," the girl smiled. "If the bear had been hungry, it would have acted in a normal manner. All I did was calm your horse."

More than that the girl refused to say and Dusty found himself involved in a discussion about the cattle industry. Not until laying in his blankets did he realise that he had not asked any of the questions puzzling him about his companions. Then the thought struck him that every time he made his mind up to obtain the answers to his questions about the travellers, he found himself involved in a discussion which left him no opportunity to satisfy his curiosity.

Over breakfast, Vaza asked that she be allowed to spend a day in the valley so as to see the eggs hatch out. Dusty agreed, mainly to please her, but also because the team horses showed signs of strain after their hard pushing of the previous afternoon.

For once in his life Dusty relaxed and lost his alertness when away from the safe confines of the OD Connected ranch house. There seemed to be an air of unreality in the peace of the valley. Three times during the day, he saw the grizzly in or around the clearing, but none of the horses showed the slightest concern and the bear ignored them and the men.

At first Dusty worried about the girl going alone out of sight of the camp, but she insisted. Thinking on how she handled the bear, Dusty's fears soon died away and he lounged in the camp, taking things easy.

The late afternoon sun shone down on the peaceful valley and Dusty sat with Adek at the table while Jarrel emerged from the wagon. Seeing two shapes rise from the bushes, Dusty began to thrust back his chair. Although the shapes wore range clothing, Dusty knew that they were nothing so innocent as chance-passing strangers. Neither looked like a half-breed or showed signs of being wounded, so they would be Buck-Eye Baise and Tom Moon, least illustrious of the four escaped prisoners.

"Just set still, feller," the taller of the newcomers ordered. "And don't reach for a gun."

"Happen you look over that ways a piece, you'll see why," the second went on.

Obeying the man's suggestion, Dusty looked and what he saw caused him to release the butt of his gun and sink down into his chair. Vaza came from the bushes closely followed by a tall, slim man with a handsome face and wearing rumpled, trail-dirty but expensive clothing of the style worn on the Texas-Mexican border. One arm locked about the girl's waist, the other held the blade of a knife across her throat. Sick with anxiety, Dusty knew that Vaza had fallen into the clutches of Javelina.

For the first time in his life Dusty felt completely helpless. Given but a split second, he could draw and shoot; but not while Javelina held the knife to the girl's throat. The expression of terror on Vaza's face held Dusty in check and shocked him. After seeing her face the grizzly bear, he could not conceive her being afraid. Then Dusty knew the reason. Vaza's powers were of no use against the most ruthless, merciless animal of all—man.

Dusty bore no antipathy towards any race, creed or skin color—the Ysabel Kid, who Dusty had risked his life to save on more than one occasion, had a Comanche grandfather—but he knew that few men were more

devoid of human feeling than half-breeds of Javelina's
blood-line. Without a single hesitation, the man would
kill Vaza and never give a thought to her being a girl.

"Stand up slowly, cow-nurse," Javelina ordered, his
face a happy mask which did not fool Dusty and
brought about instant obedience. "Now take off the
gunbelt and toss it aside."

Having come to his feet, Dusty unbuckled the gunbelt
and tossed it away from him. He knew that doing so
meant death, but so did refusal and while alive he could
still hope for a chance. Already the taller of the men had
picked up his carbine and worked the lever to ensure
that its breech held a bullet.

"Go fetch him, Buck-Eye," Javelina ordered as
Dusty's gunbelt landed.

"I'll just get me them guns," answered the shorter of
the man.

"Do what I said!" hissed the half-breed. "He might
die any minute and we don't want that—at least, not
until after he tells us where he hid the money."

"Jav's right, Buck-Eye," commented the third member of the escaped trio, handling the carbine with casual
ease. "We've got this bunch corralled now."

Apparently Javelina did not wish to find himself the
only member of the trio without a firearm. Equally he
used an argument for obedience that both his companions could understand.

"All right," Baise growled, hovering over the belt.
"I'll leave it, but don't neither of you touch it while I'm
gone."

"Don't you trust us, Buck-Eye?" purred Javelina.

"I trust you—as much as you trust me. Which same
I'll just take me one of these plough-handles in case I
run into any wild Injuns."

Bending, the man drew the Colt from the left holster,

glanced down to check that it had percussion caps on the nipples, then placed it into his waistband. Although a grin twisted Javelina's lips, it did not reach his eyes; but he made no comment as Baise walked back into the bushes.

"Get food and coffee, old man," the half-breed ordered.

"What do you want with us?" asked Adek, his voice faltering. "We have———"

"I said get food," Javelina replied and the knife moved from Vaza's throat to place its point against her cheek. "Or do I have to show you her blood."

"Do as he says, Adek," Dusty said.

"Release the girl, she has done you no harm," the old man groaned.

"No," admitted the half-breed, "and you can't do any while I hold her. The word is that you're a good doctor, *hombre*. Don't argue. Buck-Eye was in Linton last night looking to steal horses and guns. He heard about you and came straight back to us. I never expected him to show that much good sense."

"I know a little about medicine," Adek said.

"Then I've something for you to do."

"He saved that cowhand's life, but I don't reckon he knows how to dig a bullet out of a man," Dusty put in.

"You're smart, cow-nurse," Moon growled. "Got it all figured out who we are and what we want. For a short-growed r———"

"That's right, Tom boy," Javelina grinned. "Make the most of it and be real thankful that he can't get to you. I recognise him now. That's Dusty Fog."

"Him?"

"Him. I'm right, aren't I, Cap'n Fog?"

"You're right," Dusty answered as the knife made a

tiny gesture towards Vaza's face. "And the Kid and Mark Counter are close at hand."

"A good try," the half-breed said. "You're alone. We've been trailing you all day and know that."

"I will cook you food," Jarrel remarked, but he lacked training in the game of poker and gave warning to the alert half-breed.

"Go to it," Javelina answered. "Only we'll eat one at a time and the first hint that anything's wrong, this girl won't look pretty any more."

"What happens to Adek and the others if he gets Tetley well enough to talk?" asked Dusty.

"What do you think?"

"You've everything you want here. Take it and leave them be."

"I may just do that," grinned the half-breed.

"You mean to kill us after I have served my purpose," Adek informed him. "So if I refuse———"

"I'll start carving the girl's face to pieces," the half-breed finished.

"What would your Cousin Betty do, Dusty?"

Vaza's eyes locked with Dusty's and he could hear her words, although her lips never moved and the other gave no sign of knowing she spoke. During one of their nightly discussions, Dusty had told how he learned the deadly techniques of karate and ju jitsu from his Uncle Devil's Japanese servants and mentioned that his cousin, Betty Hardin, also gained some proficiency in the Oriental bare-hand fighting arts.

Automatically Dusty's mind mapped out a course of action. Not that he had any intention of telling Vaza. The risks would be too great, even discounting the fact that he could hardly explain without arousing Javelina's suspicions.

Almost as the thoughts came to Dusty, Vaza followed them; acting as if he spoke aloud. Giving a frightened gasp, she went limp and sagged against Javelina's left arm which encircled her waist and pinned down her own arms to her sides. From what he had seen of the travellers, Javelina experienced no surprise when he felt the girl collapse as if in a faint and he relaxed, allowing the knife to move away from her cheek.

"Do———!" Dusty began to yell, knowing the deadly peril Vaza's moves entailed. While his Cousin Betty might have brought off the move, given the inducement of certain death awaiting no matter whether she obeyed or not, Vaza lacked the training.

Inexperienced or not, Vaza acted correctly, following Dusty's thought pattern exactly. She took a long step forward with her left foot and by bending her knees lowered her body in the grasping arm. By suddenly raising her arms, she freed herself, knocking Javelina's encircling arm upwards. Before the half-breed realised what had happened, Vaza pivoted slightly and smashed back her elbow, driving it hard into his solar plexus.

Dusty wasted no time in yelling more than the two letters. Whichever way things went, he knew that only one course remained open to him. Already Baise approached through the bushes, leading a horse which trailed a travois that bore the fourth member of the escaping party. However, Dusty hoped that the man might be too far away to take a hand in the proceedings during their vital opening stage. Moon expected no trouble, certainly not a reaction as swift as the girl's, and stared in her direction, the carbine still across the crook of his arm.

Going forward in a rolling dive, Dusty caught up his remaining Colt in passing. A jerk slid the holster free and sent the belt flying. Then he came to his knees, edge of his left hand chopping back the hammer of the Colt in his right and fanning off a shot. While fanning could not be termed an accurate way of shooting, a skilled man could plant a bullet on a big enough target at reasonable ranges. Dusty possessed that skill and his lead drove into Moon's belly even as the man tried to swing free the carbine. Having taken the most pressing menace out of the game, while Jarrel sprang towards Moon with hands reaching for the carbine, Dusty twisted to face Javelina. What he saw drove all cohesive thought from Dusty's head. Fighting man's instincts made him deal with the most immediate danger, but they deserted the small Texan from that moment.

While Vaza's attack freed her, she lacked the ability to put all her weight behind the elbow blow; and Javelina was tough as a hickory rail. Although he took a pace to the rear, he neither lost his hold of the knife nor suffered any serious effect. So, while free, Vaza could not get far enough from the man to be safe.

With a roar of rage, the half-breed flung himself forward. He knew he was going to die and wanted to take his revenge. There would be no chance of reaching Dusty, so Javelina struck at the nearest person—Vaza. Around lashed the half-breed's knife arm in the terrible back-hand slash so favored in a fight. Even as Dusty lunged upright, firing as he did, he saw a crimson gash open in Vaza's throat and blood gush from a wound that would be fatal.

Just in instant too late Dusty's bullet caught Javelina. It knocked the man backwards, but the damage had already been done and Vaza collapsed to the ground. Mad with grief and rage, Dusty ignored the sight of Baise rushing forward and raising the Colt. Four more times Dusty fired, ripping the bullets into Javelina's reeling body, oblivious of the fact that any one of them would have killed the man.

In the violent reaction at seeing Vaza's fate, Dusty ignored the warning his subconscious mind screamed to him. While he emptied his gun into Javelina, Baise lined the Colt on him. Jarrel held the carbine, swinging around to face Baise, but the outlaw figured on Dusty being the more dangerous and made no change in his aim. Flame licked from the Army Colt's barrel even as Dusty sent the fifth bullet into the doll-rag torn body of the half-breed. Something struck Dusty on the side of the head and burning pain knifed through him. Through the whirling agony mists, he saw Jarrel line and fire the carbine, Baise jerk under the impact of a flat-nosed .44 bullet, let the Colt fall and drop. Then Dusty saw the girl's body on the ground, a growing red pool soiling the golden blonde hair.

"Vaza!" he shouted as the scene blurred and pitched before his eyes.

Then everything went black.

CHAPTER SIXTEEN

A Dream?

Dusty woke lying in his bedroll. For a moment he remained still, eyes blinking at the morning sun. Then memories flooded back to him and he jerked himself erect.

"Vaza!" he began. "Va———"

Near by the embers of the fire showed black and cold, his own coffeepot—unused during the trip from Bainesville—standing by it. To one side the paint, its feet hobbled, grazed peacefully.

But nothing more.

No wagon and team horses. No sign of Javelina, Moon, Tetley or Baise's bodies. No Adek, Jarrel or Vaza. Not even a sign of the blood which had been shed in the clearing.

Thinking of blood brought another thought to Dusty. Reaching up his hand, he touched the side of his head. No bandage or furrow of bullet-lacerated flesh met his exploring fingers, only hair and flesh apparently untouched by lead.

"What the hell?" he breathed.

Unable to think what might have happened since he collapsed unconscious, Dusty went over every inch of the clearing in a desperate search to find some proof of the fight. Not a sign remained, only the tracks of his paint and those he would have made while setting up a camp for himself. Failing to find any mark that the wagon should have left, Dusty took out first one Colt from his holster, then the other, and found both to be fully loaded, clean, showing no sign of recent use.

Running his fingers through his hair, Dusty stood for a moment and looked around the clearing. Slowly he returned to the dead fire and gave way to a nagging thought at the back of his mind.

"A dream?" he said. "Could it all have been a dream?"

Yet it had all seemed so real. He could remember every detail—or could he? Memories stirred in his head, thoughts of a lonely ride overland after leaving the town of Bainesville, and something inside him seemed to be telling him that nobody could do the things which Adek, Jarrel and Vaza did. People could not read each other's thoughts as the trio appeared to do. No company in the United States had managed to put up meals which required only heating to be ready to serve. Horseshoes wore out, which those of the wagon team showed no signs of doing. So many other things could not have happened.

Slowly Dusty returned to his bedroll and began to pack it. Bent's Ford lay a day's hard ride away—it would have been longer accompanying a wagon—and he decided to waste no time in reaching the hospitable place. With the coffeepot packed, bedroll strapped into place. Dusty freed and saddled the paint. Just as he swung into the saddle, his paint gave an explosive snort and showed signs of nervousness. Looking around, Dusty saw a bear rise among the bushes across the clearing. A big grizzly bear with a ragged, bullet-torn left ear. Only for a moment did it stare, then it acted as he might expect it to under the circumstances. There could be only one or two natural reactions; either the bear would charge, or run. With a sigh of relief, Dusty saw the grizzly choose the latter. Giving an explosive "whoof!" it turned and crashed away through the bushes.

"What the hell did I expect?" he mused as he started the paint moving. "It must have been a dream."

It would be many years before the first author wrote fiction, or prophesied facts, about the possibility of travel between planets and through space. Dusty had therefore nothing to lead him to believe that such a thing be possible and knew nothing of beings from another world, possibly much further advanced scientifically than his own. Nor had he ever heard of post-hypnotic suggestion; planting an idea in the subconscious so that it became accepted as a fact.

So, while everything appeared to have been so real, he accepted the growing thought that he had only dreamt of meeting the travellers. If he had gone over the rim into the next valley, he might have found further cause for confusion and uncertainty. At the foot of the slope, a great round patch of blackened earth and vegetation showed that recently some searing heat had been applied.

Night had fallen when Dusty led his leg-weary paint, as was the privilege of an old friend, into Duke Bent's private stables. While he cared for the horse, he heard the doors open and, turning, found Mark Counter and the Ysabel Kid approaching.

"You're a day late," the Kid accused. "Who was the girl? Or are you going to try to tell us that you went out with a posse after those four prisoners who escaped on the way to Fort Smith?"

"Four prisoners?" Dusty repeated.

"Vic Tetley, Buck-Eye Baise, Tom Moon and my good old amigo Javelina," explained the Kid. "Haven't you heard about it?"

"If you haven't," Mark drawled, "just where've you been?"

Dusty sucked in a long breath and did not reply for some time. At last he shook his head and said, "Maybe I'll never know."